THE
NIGHT
CONTRACT

A *LANCE GEDRIN* MYSTERY

GREG
GOUNTANIS

RB
ROWDY BOOKS

Published by Rowdy Books

Ebook ISBN: 978-1-953762-02-3

Paperback ISBN: 978-1-953762-00-9

Cover design by Deranged Doctor Design

First edition: November 2020

THE LANCE GEDRIN SERIES

The Night Contract (Lance Gedrin #1)

The Fink (Lance Gedrin #2)

The Loran (Lance Gedrin #3)

The Jobber (Lance Gedrin #4)

The Lance Gedrin Box Set (Books 1-4)

1

When I got my walking papers from Pontiac Correctional I barged into Judo's Diner faster than a junkie on speed. I ate mushy silver dollar pancakes, soggy scrambled eggs, and extra salty bacon on the side. The regulars called it a coronary dilemma. But having not experienced civilization for the last twelve years, I called it muy bueno. Non-plasticky, non-rubbery, non-Styrofoam-y bliss. Even though I was more of an omelet aficionado, my taste buds knew there was room for compromise. I wolfed the comida down in six minutes flat, and I topped it all off with a big glass of OJ. The waitress gave me a fortune cookie for dessert. *The fortune you seek is another cookie.* I asked for seconds, but Judo was gone and had them under lock and key. No bueno.

I paid the bill in quarters and left a customary tip. Then I found the nearest bus station and took a Greyhound to Blackfoot, Idaho. When you're seconds away from getting a three-drug cocktail that will stop your heart permanently for a murder you didn't commit, things become crystal clear. And when you live to tell the tale, something's gotta give. My lawyer Gertrude Stevenson called it a new lease on life. "Take advantage of your freedom," she said. "While you still have it." I'm normally allergic to authority figures and take what they have to say with at least three grains of salt, but Stevenson was right. I was starting a new chapter, but my case was far from over. Even though I was freed on appeal and granted bail with permission to travel, the ball was in the State of Illinois's court now. With my murder conviction officially reversed and the case remanded back to the trial court for further proceedings, they could either retry me, give me a kick-ass deal if I pleaded guilty, or toss the bullshit case once and for all.

The odds never favored ex-cons so I made a bucket list. My first stop was the Idaho Potato Museum. I needed fiber in my life and needed to honor an old deputy who'd snuck me Pringles from time to time. The potato capital of the world was sublime.

Admission was six bucks. The 5,500-square-foot building first opened its doors in 1988. I took the tour and learned that the first potato came to the States in the 1700s. I followed the exhibits closely and learned how farmers cultivated the fields and harvested the famous potatoes. I skipped the potato science experiment modules, but thoroughly enjoyed the potato-themed film at the end. All in all, I spent two hours in the museum and ten minutes in the gift shop. I even bought a potato key chain that said "Pure Idaho." On the way out, I stopped at the cafe and had a baked potato filled with butter. My stomach got an A for adjusting seamlessly to real food, across state lines. I wondered how it would fare on finer cuisine and exotic delicacies and made a note to experiment later.

I found a local watering hole and an hour later walked out with a purple-haired poet girl. I needed a motel, and the poet girl needed a bathroom. In another life I wanted five-star amenities and scenic views, but not in this one. I found a place seven minutes away and paid cash. Sadly, the Illinois Department of Corrections does not give you a severance package upon release. My net worth consisted of a black coffee-stained t-shirt, a ripped pair of blue jeans, and sneakers that were popular the last time the Knicks were good. If I added the peanuts in my wallet, I could get through several nights, but eventually I needed to become a productive citizen in el mundo.

I plopped down on the rickety bed and the poet girl found the bathroom. I didn't think I'd get much sleep given the circumstances, but I tested different spots on the bed. For a sideways sleeper, the angles made all the difference between a healthy dose of shuteye and yet another bout with insomnia. Left, right, forty-five degrees. I tried every possible configuration and realized I needed another perspective.

"Do you want the window side or the fridge side?" I asked the poet girl as she came out of the bathroom.

She ignored me and took all her clothes off. I didn't ask any more questions. We tested the durability of the bed for hours. It's amazing how clear your mind is when nobody is coming to shank you in the middle of the night. Ultimately, the poet girl took the fridge side, and I took the window side. I was wide awake, so I scrolled through the exquisite cable package the motel offered. A football game. A boxing match. A telenovela. The squared circle won out. It was in my blood. Two uninspired heavyweights threw wobbly punches in a half-empty arena.

They sucked, and I could do much better straight out the joint.

There was a knock at the door.

"*Periodico*," the cleaning lady said, handing me a copy of *USA Today*.

The boxing analysts decried the fight. The crowd wanted a refund. I wondered if the motel always delivered papers at nighttide. I flipped through the paper, back to front. Starting with sports, then arts, then weather, then the headlines.

When I got to the first page, my whole life changed.

2

Stevenson's diablo-red curls filled the page like fine wine. The headline read, "High-Profile Defender Goes Missing." Underneath the bold letters, Stevenson stood on the courthouse steps, hands raised in victory. Another shot of another win. She did that a lot. My bad ass lawyer kicked ass and got every trophy. Stevenson was the Michael Jordan of criminal defense lawyers.

Or she had been. She hadn't been seen in five days.

I spread the paper out on the bed and read the whole article in two minutes. My brain kept going back to last week, when Stevenson sat across from me at Pontiac and told me I was getting out. Two days before she vanished.

"The first district vacated your conviction," Stevenson said. "They remanded back to the trial court, and now the state has to get their ass in line and figure out if they're going to take another shot at this bullshit case. I filed an emergency motion for bond. No judge is stupid enough to deny it under the circumstances." Before I could let out the waterworks, she added, "It's over. Move on with your life, champ."

The words stuck to me like Gorilla Glue and never went out of style. And just like that I was back on the outside looking for pancakes. I owed my life to Stevenson. She believed in my innocence when nobody else would. She saw through the bull-shit and went to war. She never left my corner and went twelve rounds with all the crooked cops, lawyers, and judges.

Stevenson was family.

And I wanted answers.

I flipped to one of the news channels. Sure enough, she was the top story. A bunch of talking heads debated whether foul play was involved. The consensus was Stevenson had a lot of demons doing difficult work. She had a history of depression and anger management problems. She'd gone through a bitter divorce. She popped one too many Ambiens. I watched for an hour and wanted to knock out all the suits on screen. They wore too much makeup and didn't have a damned clue. Stevenson made life her bitch every second of every day. She relished fighting for the underdog and wouldn't hang it up unless she got life without parole.

The poet girl stirred next to me, moaning and reaching for my outstretched hand on the bed. I played dead and after a few seconds she pulled away. Si. Maybe she'd publish an anthology one day or tag murals in her neighborhood for the aesthetic release. I wouldn't be around to see it, but I would be in spirit like I was with all the female companions who floated in and out of my life like a bout of influenza. Down the line all roads led somewhere important. I had no idea what or where or when or how, but one day it would all hit me in the face. I just hoped for a concussion-free experience.

I hopped off the bed and knocked out some pushups. I did a hundred every morning out of habit to get the blood flowing. I shut the TV and packed my things. It took me thirty-three seconds to get everything together.

The poet girl got up, rubbed her eyes, and smiled.

"I'm going to Chicago," I said.

When I checked out, the motel keeper was so paranoid about a bad review that he offered me a free night.

The keeper said, "You don't like the bed? I get you a new room. Suite on other side. Extra night on the house. No Yelp bad for me please."

I said, "No, amigo."

The keeper relented. "Where you go?"

"The Windy City."

The keeper's face lost color. "Very big place. Very dangerous. I got carjack one time when I go to visit my sister. Lot of crime and bad people. They no catch those guys. Police do nothing. Watch out."

I could have changed my mind about the free night right then and there. I could have tested the durability of the suite mattress and the poet girl could have read me her best lines. But I had unfinished business. I thanked the keeper for his hospitality and went back to the bus terminal. I sat on the same bench at the same spot as when I first landed in Blackfoot. I crossed the potato museum off my bucket list. If anybody asked, I'd say the museum was a phenomenal experience. I'd recommend it to those passing through the area, and I'd give them coupons for the gift shop.

But Chicago was muy differente.

The keeper was right, but Stevenson deserved better.

3

Thirty-eight hours later I was glaring at Howie Carton's mug. He was in the airplanes section of the Harold Washington Library, shelving four books a pop. I didn't have a Chicago Public Library card, but I wasn't checking out. I was checking in. With Carton. A geriatric con once told me that humans married above or below their station. One ruled the roost while the other played possum. The struggle was real.

Carton married way above his station.

And Stevenson knew it because she never took his name and divorced him three months into the marriage.

I wasn't a rocket scientist, but common sense said that ex-husbands were suspect numero uno when their former paramours went missing. They had all the motive and all the opportunity. Stevenson always complained about Carton during our visits on the inside. *He doesn't take out the trash. He loves those damned non-fiction books. He thinks minimum wage is cool. He's got this squinty scowl that pisses me off.* I'd sit there and nod my head at all the right times and frown at all the others.

Carton was the ultimate freeloader, but somehow he'd captured Stevenson's heart.

At first glance, I couldn't see why. Carton's wavy brown hair, coke bottle glasses, and gray jeans with suspenders clashed with his green polo and plastic nametag that read "Hi, I'm Howie." No bueno. But for now I'd give the hombre some credit. Maybe he'd read all the books on seduction. And maybe he'd dissected every variable in the love game and bagged an alpha female.

I picked up a model submarine book. The fine print made me nauseous, but the pictures were muy bueno. I analyzed the book while Carton shelved. The plan was simple. I'd ask a question, then Carton would answer it. Then he'd ask a question, and I'd answer it. The mutual questioning would go on until one of the parties got tired or something was revealed that shouldn't have been. A golden nugget. That's what I wanted. A clean victory with no migraines. I'd employ this plan not just with Carton, but on the rest of my travels till I got answers about Stevenson's disappearance.

Carton shelved four more books. He smiled and whistled while he worked. If I had to peg the tune, I'd say it was bluesy with a dash of folksy. Carton was one of them Southern boys.

A few seconds later he reached my shelf and said, "Pardon me, mister." He picked up five books this time.

I said, "If you harmed a hair on Gertrude's head, pardon me for weighing my options."

Carton's eyes widened and he dropped all the books in his hand. They survived the fall, spinal integrity intact.

"I already spoke to the detectives last week," he said. "Leave me alone." He picked up the books and shelved them.

I wasn't letting him get off that easy. I gave him my model submarine book. "This was sticking out. Don't know where it belongs, hombre."

Carton furrowed his brows, then held his hand out for the book. I gave it to him and pretended to browse for more. Carton found the right spot for the submarine book in a heartbeat. Then he came back to me.

"Who do you work for?" he asked.

"Humankind," I said.

"Bullshit. Everybody reports somewhere."

"I do have good rapport with a motel keeper in Idaho."

Carton smiled. "Sounds about right. With that getup." He eyed my faded ensemble.

I smiled. "I've been indisposed for a while, junior. I came all the way here to ask you a very important question."

Carton rolled his eyes.

"Pancakes or waffles?" I asked.

Carton laughed so hard he almost pulled an oblique. "Neither. I like oatmeal."

I shook my head, then Carton parked his cart in between aisles and led me to a vacant study room. We took chairs at a wooden table. I stretched my neck out in a million different directions. My body'd been through a lot of trauma over the years, but I was still ticking.

"My lawyer told me not to speak to anybody," Carton said. "There's an ongoing investigation, man."

I respected the lawyer's advice, but one of the great things about not being in law enforcement was that the rules didn't apply to me. Things like probable cause and reasonable suspicion and warrants. Nada. I was free to investigate the shit outta whatever I wanted, whenever I wanted.

I said, "You expecting to go down for it?"

"No."

"Then who gives a shit?" I held Carton's eyes for a few seconds, then he relented. Damn, I still had game.

"Who the hell are you?"

"The guy that's gonna make you remember this conversation the rest of your life."

Carton closed his eyes for a long time. The gears were churning in his head. Some buff stranger comes in guns blazing like that and what do you do? What's the play that will save your ass, but still make you look macho?

"We were on two different chapters," Carton said. "I was on the first, she was on the tenth. We could never quite meet."

"Too much Tomb Raider," I said.

Carton shook his head. "Too much cheating."

Carton told me everything. Her faults, not his. Stevenson cheated every second of every day. She'd be gone for days at a time working on special projects. Her contacts were filled with hundreds of men she never once mentioned. She'd go weeks without a single phone call. They shared a bed on their wedding night and their post-wedding morning. No honeymoon.

Carton teared up a little, and I felt for the guy. It would take time getting used to having the whole bed to yourself, but it definitely had its perks. But the more I listened to him, the more confused I was. A shelver dude leaving a legendary attorney? Throwing away all the money on the table? It didn't sit right.

I said, "That's one tall tale."

Carton said, "The truth kicks you in the ass sometimes."

"People never shelve their books in the right places."

"You never answered my question. Who the fuck are you?"

I told him. The bare minimum. First name and last name. No other particulars.

Carton nodded. "Ah, I knew you'd come around. Gertrude busted her ass for you. Working non-stop to make sure you had a life. And where did that get her?" He made a poof motion with his hands.

"She busted her ass for me, so I'm busting my ass for her. I'm not stopping till I find out everything."

"If you wanna find the sick fuck who did this, follow the trail," he said.

"Where?"

"*Follow the trail*, man. How stupid are you?"

I'd had a lot of concussions in my day, but it usually didn't interfere with getting things done. I found the answer eventually. But this one stumped me.

"Find her bedroom cowboys," Carton said, "and you'll find what you're looking for."

"That list is longer than my cuticles," I said.

He shook his head. "The bangers. She rolled with them. She double-crossed them, and they did her in."

"Who?" I asked.

"The Serbians."

Before I could ask anything else, a patron walked in and asked for help finding a book, and Carton went back to the stacks, leaving me alone with my golden nugget.

———

SOMEBODY MUST HAVE LOVED FUCKING with me, because when I left the library I passed a law school. I was tempted to stop in and observe a daily dose of shyster training before I proceeded with my mission, but I didn't want to upend the rhythm of the aspiring public pretenders.

Carton's words were a great start. Leads meant trails and trails meant possibilities. He'd pointed me forward, and I'd follow till the path went cold. I walked toward Michigan Avenue trying to ignore the hubbub of traffic. My lungs welcomed the Chicago humidity for a few seconds, then protested. The daily dose of PTSD aside, one of the perks of living in a shoebox surrounded by bars is that minor daily stresses don't exist. What to wear. What to eat. What car to drive. What to say to your nosy neighbor. Life moved fast on the outside, and I needed to adjust—rapido. Once a con, always a con never sat straight with me like it did with the rest of society.

I crossed a bridge, and the traffic went down a decibel. Stevenson's firm was ten minutes away in the heart of River North. If the background shots flanking the reporters on TV were accurate, the building made Blackfoot look like one of those annoying water bugs you squash with the heel of your shoe.

Stevenson lived and worked in style.

But somebody didn't share Stevenson's taste. I wasn't officially crossing Carton off my list, but he didn't seem good for it. The shelver homicide? Nah. I knew that time was of the essence. Stevenson had been missing several days now and any *Law & Order* aficionado knew that a missing person case quickly became a murder case after the first forty-eight hours. I hoped for the best, but expected the worst.

I crossed another bridge and was close. I ran the street names in my head again and again. The experts said that adjusting to the outside could take years, if it ever happened at all. I'd learned all this from the hundreds of books I devoured on the inside. The inmates called me "the Professor" because I couldn't stop reciting random factoids. If you're feeling stressed, try some deep breathing. Think happy thoughts and your brain composition will change. You catch feelings for that chick you banged at the club before you got locked up? That's oxytocin, bro. I cited the best block quotes from all the dog-eared pages. I didn't get any awards, but I got a quick wit that I wasn't afraid to use. It got me in trouble mucho, but it also got me out of trouble mucho. Some called it hubris. I called it coping. One day at a time, hombre.

I approached the Mag Mile and realized that my potato farm look wouldn't fly at a fancy firm. I needed a new wardrobe, one that would appease not only all the fine motel keepers in the world, but all the suits too. I left Pontiac with an olive t-shirt on the fritz, ripped jeans, sneakers, a wallet with an expired ID card, and a Daffy Duck watch. Add the potato key chain from the museum and the backpack I'd bought at one of the bus stops along the way, and that made seven possessions in my new life. Eight if you counted the ID card and wallet as two items. Nine if you counted the dwindling cash in my wallet.

I needed at least eleven items to be on top of my game.

I found a Macy's a block away and went to the men's department. I found the clearance section and took my time. Believe it or not, before my fall from grace, I was quite the fashionista. I occupied myself with selecting the perfect hue of denim and slim-cut dress shirts. I once had a bustling closet of monk-strap shoes, wingtips, and oxfords. Now, I had to stretch the couple hundred bucks left from my prisoner property as far as humanly possible. Stevenson promised me a settlement from the city once the case was all over. I called bullshit, but lawyers have a way of making everything sound right. The state could've dropped my case the minute I got out, but all appearances indicated they'd fight till the bitter end rather than admit they took twelve birthdays away from someone for no reason at all. The appellate court gave them ten days to decide whether to retry me. Seven days down. Three to go.

Nada. All quiet on the western front.

Whatever. I really wanted some new jeans. After circling the same aisle four times, I went with Levis 511s and a light-blue V-neck tee. After an eternity in the shoe section, I finished with a pair of brown suede Chelsea boots. They were so comfortable and they stood up well on the streets. All in all, I spent thirty minutes shopping and forty-four seconds changing into my new clothes. I had twelve worldly possessions now, not eleven, but I took comfort in the fact that I had a hundred bucks to spare. One hell of a sale.

I passed the Bean at Millennium Park and the bridge where the Chicago River was dyed green every year for Saint Patrick's Day. Stevenson's firm was a stone's throw away. I started with the ex-husband and now I'd penetrate the inner circle. Motive was powerful.

When I found the firm, news vans lined the whole block. Satellites stretched into the sky like cathedral spires as all the networks prepped for prime time. The sharks were out in full force, and they weren't letting up. As I got closer, I noticed one of the reporters from one of the more contentious segments on TV. She was a petite Asian brunette, and she was stunning. She played with her phone as people did her hair and makeup. She was a boss.

But not mine.

I said, "My lawyer didn't bite the bullet."

4

The reporter said, "Pride comes before the fall." She looked up from her phone and I realized the camera didn't do her justice. She was muy guapa.

But I wouldn't let her get off that easy. "She never expressed any suicidal thoughts. She came from a balanced home. She had a Doberman named Henri." Stevenson got him as a puppy from an old lady who couldn't take care of him anymore, and every time she came to visit me on the inside she showed me pictures of Henri's growth. At his last checkup, Henri weighed a solid eighty-eight pounds of pure muscle.

The reporter smiled, and I couldn't tell if it was one of those flirty smiles or one of those you-got-me smiles. "Pull back the curtain. People are pretty fucked up behind closed doors." She put her hand out. "Erin Stine. Nice to meet you, Professor."

My mandible would have hit the floor if it wasn't connected to my maxilla. Reporters were annoying types, but a select few were both annoying and good. Real good. Stine was in the upper echelon no matter how you sliced it. How many hands did she grease to find out I was the Professor? And how did she know I'd be in the right place at the right time to school me with it?

"When did they give stalkers media credentials?" I asked.

Stine laughed and playfully punched my shoulder. "I saw you walking on State. You take up the whole damned sidewalk with those triceps. And our station got a Snapchat of you picking up clothes from the clearance rack. Looks like the badass heavyweight champ still has some fans out there."

Stine must have been speaking in code because I was confused as hell. Why would a chat snap? One thing was clear though: I may have kicked ass and taken names before the fall, gracing magazine covers, commercials, and primetime TV, but now I was pathetic. I wasn't in Idaho, but the more things changed the more things stayed the same. Bigger city. Same problems. Nobody recognized me anymore. Nobody gave a shit. Except for the snapper chatter.

Stine went back to her phone. "Do you mind sitting for an exclusive?"

"No way."

"I think it can really help shape the narrative of what's going on with Gertrude."

"There's no narrative. Somebody got too cute, and I'm going to find out who."

Stine looked up from her phone. "And when you find them, what are you going to do about it?"

"What I always do." I let the words hang, and sure enough Stine took the bait. She pulled out a mini-notepad from her pocket and scribbled away. I had been around reporters long enough to know that they lived for the sound bite and they salivated for the exclusive. They chased them the way a struggling actor chased the next casting call. I was Stine's ticket to the big leagues, to the city that never sleeps.

And Stine was my ticket to getting answers. I enjoyed the tango.

I said, "What time did she go missing?"

Stine said, "Gertrude worked late on the twenty-fourth, then did your bond hearing the next morning. Hell of a job because you got out. She went silent around noon. Partners were trying to congratulate her. She sent one of those form texts back saying thanks...and then crickets. When the whole office showed up to work the next morning and she wasn't in, the whispers started. They called it in midday."

"Who did the honors?"

"One of the associates at the firm."

"Have you crossed her yet?"

"This isn't a courtroom." Stine hollered at one of the camera guys behind her.

"The only way to test somebody's recollection is to stress them out. Fuck with their mind a little. If they're lying, they won't be able to hide."

"I didn't know you got a degree in law enforcement on the inside."

The professor knows all, missy. Including the Serbian bangers connection. But I played my cards close to the chest. "How many people work at the firm?" I asked.

"At least fifty. Maybe seventy if you count all the secretaries and janitors." Stine went back to her phone, and I wondered if I could get one and still have enough for a bus ride cross country.

I said, "That's at least seventy suspects. How many have you interviewed?"

Stine said, "Nobody has gone on record. Camera or print. The partners are keeping a tight leash on this thing. They released a statement with a bunch of platitudes. The usual bullshit. The firm's statement: 'We are confident in the authori-

ties handling of this matter and pledge our complete coopera-
tion.' Complete silence since then."

"Give me a name."

"That's gonna cost ya." Stine smiled again, this time much
flirtier.

"My commissary account got raided. I've allotted twenty
dollars and seventy cents for miscellaneous expenses. Take it or
leave it."

"Let's make a deal." Stine walked back to the cameraman
and sat in one of those tall director's chairs. A makeup lady
went to work.

"Depends on the terms," I said.

"I give you the scoop, you give me the exclusive," Stine said.

"When?"

"When the time is right. This piece is going to be huge
once New York gets ahold of it."

I came for answers, and I was slowly getting them. The
papers were playing their cards close to the vest, but opportunity is muy bueno. I needed more, so I took the deal. I wasn't an
expert in contracts, but the details seemed fair enough. And if
the source dried up I'd be on the next bus to the Space Needle.
Numero dos on the bucket list.

"Sounds like a plan." I went to shake hands, but Stine gave
me her fist instead. She bumped it like we were bros and that's
how the Gedrin-Stine partnership was born.

"Gertrude ran in some tough crowds over the years. Drug
dealers. Psychos. Mobsters. She wanted more and more clients
and she was swept up in the storm. I've been on the beat here
three months and it's the dirty little secret nobody talks about."

"You're the arm of the republic. You control the story."

"I wish. I control the narrative I'm given. The talking
points. Anything doesn't jibe with the execs, it gets nixed. No
questions asked. There are so many leads that I wanna chase

down, but I can't. Losing my livelihood is not top priority right now."

"I'm no snitch. Who had it out for her?"

Stine looked all around like people were spying on her. They weren't. The live shots were about to start. She turned back to me and said, "Gertrude played with the Serbians a lot. My money's on them if you ask me."

Muy bueno. Carton. Stine. The path was hot as hell. "And the assholes are being protected."

"The rich and powerful run this place. Tale as old as time. Always have. Always will." Stine nodded to the cameraman, and I stepped back. It was the top of the hour and simultaneously a bunch of the reporters nearby took their spots.

"Who was the caller?" I said.

Stine pressed something into her ear and looked at some papers in front of her. She looked back at me and said, "Kayla Tempe."

"Excellent."

"Watch out for that one."

"Is she Serbian?"

"No."

Before I could ask more, Stine went live.

And I went inside.

5

Lawyers liked excess, and Stevenson was no different. As I got off the elevator on the fifteenth floor, the plush red carpet that greeted me made the Oscars look like amateur hour. Mahogany armchairs lined the walls like sentries guiding the way to a throne. I'd timed my visit perfectly. It was mid-afternoon which meant that court was over, and the firm was near peak capacity. A bunch of associates were trying to get the partners to remember their names, and a bunch of partners were trying to find creative ways to tell the associates that their services would no longer be needed come fall. The song and dance would go on until quitting time.

Which meant that I'd get more answers. Start at the top and go all the way to the bottom. Make a list and check it twice. I didn't know the managing partner's name, but I figured I'd start there. Time was ticking. Ask any cop, corrupt or not, and they'll tell you the early days of a missing persons investigation are crucial. Leads go cold, memories fade, phony tips pour in like Niagara Falls on steroids. All the while the perp lurks in the shadows and takes advantage of his quarry. Stevenson went missing one week ago. I was late, but I wasn't quitting. I'd go twelve rounds to find out what happened.

I walked up to the receptionist and flashed the widest smile I could. Even with all the pancakes in my life, my pearly whites were alabaster and awesome. They melted the most reserved woman all the way to the craziest alpha.

"How can I help you sir?" the receptionist asked. She had a flat affect, and I had sore orbital bones.

"I have an appointment with the managing partner."

The receptionist looked at her computer screen. "Our senior partner is unavailable. Would you like to reschedule?"

In addition to the professorial skills I'd developed on the inside, I'd become the quintessential body language expert. I could spot thieves, rapists, shankers, gamblers, smokers, drinkers, and best of all liars. One look at a declarant's posture, breathing, eyes, and fingers, and I saw it all. Any other day the receptionist would have been in the clear. Not today. The partner was in back putting golf balls into a glass cup thinking he was close to breaking a hundred. And the receptionist was helping the cause by filling the book with phantom tasks. I appreciated the teamwork, but I wasn't a mark.

"Who's the top associate?" I asked. "This is an emergency with my case."

The receptionist stared daggers right through me, but rather than debate the point she pressed a button on her phone. "Associate to reception. Associate to reception."

I thanked her and sat down. I studied the paintings on the walls, trying to figure out the motivation for each piece. I narrowed down the epoch too. Art had a way of soothing me sometimes, and I took full advantage. It went like that for three minutes before a voice said, "Sir, may I help you? I don't believe I represent you."

I turned to see a petite blonde with long curls and muscular forearms. A sleeve of tattoos lined both her biceps. She had a small diagonal scar on her left ear, and a small brown birthmark on her right. If I had to guess, her goal in life was to give the partners heartburn so often that they'd have no choice but to elevate her station.

"I'm here for Gertrude," I said.

The blonde put her hands on her hips and stared me down. The receptionist did too. Three was better company, so I did what any normal citizen would do. I stared back. We were at a standoff for an eternity, then the blonde motioned me out of my chair. She told the receptionist to hold her calls and we walked down the hall to a large conference room with open windows and wonderful views of Lake Michigan. Stevenson must have arranged the space eons ago as an homage to Henri who loved runs in the mornings. I sat opposite the window and took in the view.

"I'm Kayla Tempe, senior associate here at the firm," the blonde said. "I have to depose a physician in a DCFS case tomorrow and you're giving me a migraine. Either you're some nut job who wants free legal services or you legitimately have info on Gertrude. If that's the case, you're too late to the party."

Her left eye twitched twice, and the more she talked the more I was intrigued by what she had to say. For whatever reason, Stine wanted me to watch out, but I'd give Tempe the benefit of the doubt. She was sassy and sexy and stubborn. The perfect package.

"It's never too late," I said.

"If a missing person doesn't surface in the first seventy-two hours, then it becomes a homicide investigation. Let's not pretend here. Where were you last week, Sherlock?" More eye twitches this time. No bueno.

"I was exploring the durability of the steel bars at Pontiac," I said. "Then I had pancakes."

Tempe poured herself a glass of water from a pitcher on the table. "Ah, the indestructible Lance Gedrin. You were quite the pain in the ass over the years here. I don't think Gertrude ever got a full night's sleep after taking your case."

"The best always find a way."

One eye twitch now. Stress was a silent killer. But progress. "A con who got his brains bashed in for a living now wants to play PI. For the life of me I don't know why I went to law school sometimes."

"For the fancy shoes and to skip the line at the clerk's office." I'd been around so many lawyers in my life that I knew them better than they knew themselves. Being an asshole was in a lawyer's blood. It came with the bar card, and so did the witty banter and the constant gamesmanship. I looked forward to the ride with Tempe.

Tempe said, "I guess the ring didn't destroy all your brain cells."

I said, "Somebody put a hit on Stevenson. With all the cases she won, she picked up enemies faster than her best mile."

"Do I look like the mafia police?" Tempe got up from her chair, paying no attention to the view. Her face was flushed, but on a positive note the twitches were long gone. "If you have any concrete information on Gertrude's whereabouts or some-body's specific motive to do her harm, go to the eighteenth district. You'll be the hundredth phony waiting. I'm not going to obstruct an ongoing investigation by playing Sherlock Holmes."

The more attitude she gave the more I wanted her to stay with me. Maybe it was the forearms or maybe it was the fact that I'd been warned. Chicks dig bad boys, and bad boys dig bosses. Tempe was definitely a boss. More than Stine.

"The police won't do shit, and you know that, counselor. Even if you cry to 911."

Tempe froze for a moment and I thought I had her. Then she said, "This doctor isn't deposing himself. Go to CPD. They get a bad rap, but they are the professionals."

The proper social etiquette in this kind of situation called for the person on the other side of the table to take the hint and leave. No questions asked. No follow-up calls. No birthday invites.

But I had other plans.

I said, "Are you hungry? I know a great pizza place."

6

"You're buying," Tempe said. I'd anticipated more of a fight, but sometimes pizza with a stranger was the best medicine.

I went with Giordano's. Tempe didn't say much on the walk over. We were like two aliens on a blind date trying to find our spaceship. She made a comment about the weather being too hot for a suit, and I made a comment about a flaw in the Bean's design. It simply could not withstand a high-impact snowfall. All in all, it was a five-minute walk with zero humidity.

When we got there, Tempe chose the booth. She sat a little right of center, closer to the pepper shakers and parmesan cheese. She tucked her curls behind her ears and grabbed a menu. I didn't need a menu, but wanted to ask for hers.

A waiter filled our water and then gave us some time to order. Eventually, Tempe said, "I'm super hungry. That's the only reason I agreed to come here."

I said, "I haven't had deep dish in twelve years and fourteen days."

Tempe stared at the menu for a few more seconds, then put it down. "I'll split a pepperoni with you." She showed a hint of a smile for a fraction of a second, then frowned. She looked at her phone and started playing with it.

"Is that a Motorola?" I asked. I was genuinely curious. Being on the inside for so long had stunted my technological acumen. I had fine-tuned my wit, but I was a dinosaur when it came to all the new gadgets. Stine was speaking about snap chatters, and now Tempe's screen was lighting up like a Christmas tree. Wow.

"What planet are you from? It's an iPhone." She pointed to the big silver apple on the back. I decided that if the city ever graciously emptied their checkbook with my name on it, I'd buy a phone with all the bells and whistles. I'd call local, international, collect, and everything in between. I'd play games on it and practice my recording voice. But I wanted one with an orange on the back. It was a more succulent fruit.

Tempe picked up on it. "You don't have a phone," she said. "That's so old school."

"Rules are rules. I could have smuggled one in, but it wasn't worth going to the hole for. And I wasn't going to let people raid my commissary. Ramen is ramen."

There was an awkward silence for a moment, then the waiter came and broke it. I ordered one large pepperoni deep dish pizza and some garlic bread. I went to town on the bread, while Tempe merely poked at it. When the basket was empty, she said, " I'm sorry about your shitty life. The most recent chapter, I mean. Man, I'm an asshole. I have issues."

"I hardly noticed."

Tempe laughed for the first time. "How long did you do, officially?"

"Nada. Twelve and change if you count time in county."

Lawyers knew the lingo, and numbers were like candy to

them. Tempe had no doubt pleaded guys out to way more time in her career. She was playing me, but I was cool. "Gertrude wouldn't shut up about your case," she said. "The awesome boxer man who was wronged."

"Nobody wanted my case, but she came in guns blazing. Didn't back down. Filed every motion and argued it like her life was on the line. Now she's gone and nobody gives a shit."

Tempe was quiet for a moment, then her eyes held mine. I wanted more, but it wasn't in the cards. The pizza came, the moment passed, and I cut the slices. Tempe appreciated the gesture. It took us forever to chew all the cheese, but I wasn't complaining.

She used a knife and fork for hers, but I went for it with my hands. I refused to mix stainless steel and tomato sauce. After a few bites, she said, "Why put a hit on her now? She's been a lawyer for twenty years."

"She worked on the toughest cases, but she came up the ranks with the petty bullshit. Traffic tickets. DUIs. He-said, she-said trespassing and thefts. Walmart wasn't going to put a hit on her. It's the biggies. Take your pick. Ex-client, officer, disgruntled judge, state's attorney. Some murder case."

"A state's attorney wouldn't have the balls. The majority are fat, slow, and moronic."

"Agreed. But this goes higher up the chain. The average criminal is stupid and impulsive. The real scary ones cover their tracks and have the cash to sweep it all under the rug. I did time with them. Could be the asshole you see in court every day who gives you the shitty deals, but I wouldn't put it past someone who lost his robe either." I was enjoying the back and forth and getting the hang of investigating. Ask a question, think of possibilities, then ask another question. Maybe a PI license was in the cards someday. I'd laminate it and wave it in Tempe's face.

Tempe grabbed another slice and cut into it. "You make a compelling argument, but it fizzles out. The police think it was a weenie wagger that got to her on her running route. They're going to the media in the next few days with sketches of some sex offender from the area. Been prowling around there for a while."

I wasn't the least bit surprised. Cops usually went with the easiest way out, which meant the lead that wouldn't draw much pushback. Sex offenders were worse than murderers in the public's eye. The sketches would seal the deal.

"When the dude goes to trial and beats the case, it's going to be a real shit show. The real killer better get the hell out of dodge while they can." I wasn't spilling Carton's lead yet. No way Jose.

Tempe frowned. "The cops seem convinced. They were talking to the partners yesterday."

"Take anything they say with three grains of salt and then rinse your mouth afterwards."

Tempe took another sip of water. "Which battle is that from?" She pointed to a long, dark-brown scar that ran from my left bicep all the way to the left of my collarbone. Some called it PTSD. I called it involuntary art.

"I let the asshole take a few swipes but then it got real," I said. "The way I like it. Hands and knees and fists and teeth and bone crunching bone. No gloves. No ring. No ref. No scorecards. Weapons are for pussies. The asshole went to the medic and never came back."

Tempe went silent for a bit, then looked for the waiter. The place was filling up with the after-work crowd, and she wanted more napkins. When the waiter didn't show I told her to use the tablecloth. She looked out for any spies and went for it.

"I feel fat," she said.

The first lesson I learned in life was never to overtly

comment on a woman's physical attributes. Nothing positive. Nothing negative. Deflect. Do not engage. Do that and you stand a chance of making it out alive.

"Tell me what Stevenson was like before she vanished," I said.

Tempe stared daggers at me again and sipped her drink. "Karma's a bitch. Let it go. The sex offender is getting his come-uppance."

Tempe knew the score. Deflect on both the giving and receiving end. We sat in silence for a while. It took eight minutes to eat all the deep dish, and I regretted going with the large. I had an A in digestion before, but now I had a C minus. My stomach wasn't quite fully adjusted to real food.

Then, the gears churned in Tempe's head. "She was annoying. Would ride all the associates hard and forget their names the next day. The interns cried when they went back to class. But she was one hell of a lawyer, and she really cared about the work."

"What was she like personally?"

"I rarely hung out with her."

"When you did, what was she into?"

"Running, Netflix, the occasional trip north to her lake house. Simple shit."

"Who's her man?"

Tempe shook her head. "Since I've known her she never had a man in her life. After the divorce she didn't do dates, and the secretary always kept her book of appointments. It was super detailed. Every hour accounted for. All work, no play. No man made the cut I guess."

"Maybe she found a secluded island and left the grid."

"She was more of a homebody who didn't have much of a home. When you've been single for the last decade plus it's hard to get back out there. Lots of bad apples."

The waiter came and I paid the bill. My cash reserves were razor-thin, but I figured I had enough to take a bus northeast if the sleuthing came up empty. I could work the register at a convenience store by the beach somewhere and taunt the state while they decided my fate.

Tempe was quiet, and I thought it was the end of the line. Perhaps I should have contacted the police and let them sort it all out. My sleuthing days were over.

But Tempe said, "Wanna hang out some more? It's nice out."

Then the vultures descended.

7

The first flash pierced my left eye, but the second was kinder—it hit the pepper shakers. Tempe shielded her face as the cameras rained down on us like we were walking the red carpet. My irises were fine at the potato museum, but this was a whole other ballgame. The waiter tried shooing away the amateur paparazzi, but they were brazen. They snapped and shouted and spoke in code as the rest of the pizza place gawked. I felt like a circus animal in a cage for the hundredth performance.

"I'm very sorry," the waiter said. "We've never had this problem before."

"The deep dish was excellent," I said.

Three more waiters joined in the effort to remove the crew.

I rolled my eyes to the right, but Tempe didn't get the message. I coughed and tapped the napkin holder, and then she got it. She sipped the last drop of her water and on the count of two we hit the kitchen. The workers chastised us for coming through, then froze when they saw me. Involuntary art does that sometimes. I was tempted to ask about the secret sauce for the deep dish, but I knew I didn't have the tools to get the job done. No pizza pan. No pizza roller. And no kick-ass oven. Maybe one day the stars would align.

We found the alley out back and headed south. The amateurs were gone.

After a minute, Tempe said, "That was an interesting way to end the dining experience."

"Too many stalkers out here. I'm more of a small-town hombre."

"More like small-time. Didn't hear 'champ' once. They weren't stalkers. They were all wearing the same shirts."

In the heat of battle it's easy to forget some of the finer details among humans. Things like what color eyebrows or what texture nasal rings or what kind of lettering is attached to fabrics. But Tempe was right: they weren't my fans. The amateurs were all unified by a cause, and they all wore the same color shirts. I might not have noticed the words, but I didn't have to. They were seared in my mind better than the juiciest steaks.

"*Justice for Amy Pako.*"

My case. My guilt. That's what the shirts stood for. Thirteen years ago they were selling like hotcakes when Pako was murdered. They flooded every court hearing to intimidate the judge, and when my conviction was overturned they flashed before every camera like a swan song.

Now they were back.

"All shirts go out of style eventually," I said.

"Not if you conned the system."

"I had a real lawyer, not a public pretender."

Tempe laughed again, and I felt like I was making some headway. We had known each other all of a couple hours, but it felt like I knew her much longer. The more Tempe talked, the more I wanted to be in her orbit. We crossed over towards the lake and found the Bean. It was a quiet pre-summer night. The sun was going down and its rays glistened against the steel marvel.

I said, "The quickest way to a woman's heart is Giordano's."

Tempe said, "You're something."

We sat in silence for a moment, less like aliens now but still trying to find the motherboard.

Tempe said, "Let's split a bottle of pinot noir at my place."

I said, "The physician won't depose himself."

Tempe grinned for half a second, then the twitches came back again. She might be a boss, but I wasn't that easy. I needed to be wooed.

I said, "Tell me the strangest thing about Stevenson, and I'll consider it."

Tempe rolled her eyes, and her face got all red for a second. I was really something, but she was likely wondering how to crack me over the head with something.

Finally, she said, "She got a weird-ass tattoo recently."

"When?"

"A few days before she disappeared."

"Where?"

Tempe took a tissue out of her purse and dabbed at an invisible blemish on her face. "Right on the inside of her wrist. Funky-looking thing. You can wear a suit every day at work and that thing still stands out like a sore thumb."

"I know exactly what you mean."

Tempe furrowed her brows.

"How many does she have?" I asked.

"Just that one, as far as I know. I didn't think she was the type, but there's a first time for everything."

"Where'd she get it?"

"There's only one place that would do something like that.

Big-ass city, but one legendary artist. He's inked me multiple times. Tat virgins play it safe."

"Was Henri with her when Mr. Legend did the deed?"

"No."

"Henri is a kind fellow."

"He bit me once, but I tend to agree."

Tempe took out her phone and typed away faster than the best pianist in the Midwest. I noticed a blue bird all over her screen. I had so much to learn.

"We're six blocks away," she said.

"Must be a shady shop."

"From my place."

"A woman's got needs, but so do I. What's that bird?"

She looked like she was going to kill me. "Um. Twitter."

"Do the chats snap on there?"

"How many concussions did you get in the ring?"

"Mucho."

Tempe frowned. We walked back toward the Mag Mile. I said nothing for a few minutes and Tempe did the same. At each intersection we would look at each other like we had some secret to share, but nothing would come out. Three minutes later, she'd had enough.

"For the record, it's the weirdos like you that make this system go around," she said. "You keep us in business with the constant billables."

"Thanks for the compliment. I haven't paid a single dime to the firm."

Tempe said, "You don't pick up on social cues that well, do you?"

"Your boss is missing and you're talking about billable hours. That's fucked up."

She stared daggers at me again. We walked another half block, and then she stopped.

"Tony's Tats is the top shop in town. Ask away, Sherlock. I'm ready to crash for the night. Later."

I flashed my pearly whites. "Watson, you have all the connects. And you're a Juris Doctor. Let's do it."

Tempe looked me up and down like I had the plague.

Then she said, "Five minutes. That's it. Then I'm done."

Still got it.

I followed the neon sign.

8

I was never into tattoos. I didn't like their permanent nature or the fact that they repelled good conversation. In the ring I was surrounded by a sea of inked monsters trying to take away every working function of my body. On the inside I was immersed in warring factions of one art form over another. But on women it was a far different story. I found their tats super sexy. As I walked in with Tempe, I wondered how many hidden ones she had.

We heard the buzz of a tattoo gun all the way in back. Before I could analyze the different designs, a punk rocker kid with a nose ring greeted us.

"We close in ten minutes," he said, pointing to a crooked sign by the front door.

"How many legendary tattoo guys you have here?" I asked.

The kid rolled his eyes like he was being told to do the dishes by his mother. "You mean artists, bruh? Did you read the sign? It's Tony's shop, and he's the man here."

The kid deserved an uppercut, but that would have been too easy.

Tempe said, "Tell Tony to stop breaking needles and get his ass out here."

The kid stuck out his tongue and trudged to the back. A few seconds later the buzzing stopped. Tempe waited, hands on hips like a mother does when her kids are being rascals. I wondered how many times she'd been fully inked and if it hurt more or less with each time. I was a badass hombre, but the thought of needles going into my body by consent made me queasy.

Then a fat man in a wifebeater and biker shorts came up to the desk where the kid used to be. I didn't need to ask if he was Tony because the sleeves of tats on his arms were a walking billboard.

"The neon sign in front is missing three bulbs," I said.

Fat Tony shrugged. "Whaddya gonna do about it?"

"Admire the mosaic." I smiled, but Fat Tony wasn't amused. He looked like he was gonna choke me with those pudgy hands.

But when he turned to Tempe, he lit up. "How are you, chica? Haven't gotten any work done lately, huh? You cheating on me with that noob down the block, Javier?" He laughed.

Tempe gave him a long hug. "Forgive my friend. He's on a mission, and he's been hit far too many times in the head to succeed." She pulled out her phone and showed him the screen. I craned my neck like a flamingo, but I couldn't get a good look at it.

"I remember that one," Fat Tony said.

"Enlighten him, please," Tempe replied.

"I ink hundreds of people a week. I'm not good with memories and shit, but I'm good with the real crazy ones."

"Who?" I said.

"That tattoo your friend has on her phone. I remember it

like it was yesterday. Real fucked up, that lady. Has one hell of a mean streak. Most people want hearts or superheroes or a kid's name. That lady wanted animals and blood. Wouldn't stop going on and on about how it was her mission to preserve all animal kind. Had to tie her down almost, wouldn't sit still."

So far all I had to go on was the fact that Stevenson was an angry tat virgin and after walking out of Fat Tony's shop she wasn't anymore. A picture was worth a thousand words. I held my palm out for Tempe's phone, but she didn't budge.

"It's been five minutes," she said.

"That clock's doing the wave and needs new batteries," I said, pointing to a dilapidated piece by the register. Fat Tony winced when I called him out on it.

Tempe shook her head but dropped her phone in my palm. I pressed the buttons a few times, but couldn't figure it out. The screen was making all sorts of noises.

Fat Tony laughed. "Where'd you find this Fred Flintstone over here?"

Tempe rolled her eyes. "He's a work in progress."

The phone fixed itself a minute later, and I critiqued the picture on it. I was no expert, but the legend was right. The tattoo was hideous—it resembled some sort of animal with mismatched colors all over. At first glance it looked like an inverted fish with scaly teeth, but upon closer inspection I saw half of a shark with hooves on the bottom instead of fins. I'd come across many ink aficionados on the inside, and had learned that people express their creativity in a million ways. Never be surprised by a con's mind. From dog dedications to female remembrances to cheesy slogans that nobody in their sober mind would get, the art told a story. Oftentimes it was a really long one filled with trials and tribulations. But Stevenson's tat took the cake. It was really fucked up. To make matters worse, blood poured out of the shark's nostrils with the words "Mea Culpa."

"She was showing this off at work?" I said.

"No. I snapped it when she was napping at her desk." Tempe took her phone back.

Fat Tony pulled out a pair of reading glasses and examined some inventory. Then he removed his glasses and stared me down. "Friends of Kayla's are friends of mine. But I don't do cops. Store policy. The last thing I need is some five-ohs coming in here poking around and fucking everything up that I've worked hard for. I've got appointments booked one month straight and don't wanna sell this place to the bodega at the corner. I know *she's* not one, but man, *you* sure look like one."

It wasn't the first time somebody thought I wore the blue. Funny thing was, right after I won the title for the first time I was offered a detective role on a cop show. I did a few episodes, then quit when it threw off my training. To this day I was linked to the blue, even though they were the ones who railroaded me and made me eat bologna for twelve years. The struggle was real.

I said, "If I was a cop I'd bust in here and tear the shit out of your place looking for answers. I'd show you a bullshit warrant and I'd take names. I'd look at your cameras and your taxes and for any illegals on your payroll. I'd kick the kid's ass for asking too many questions. Then I'd go get a donut."

Fat Tony stared me down for a good minute. Staring contests brought out the best in me, so I obliged him.

Then it was over. Fat Tony nodded. "Maybe this will help your mission, dude. The art is Serbian. They have a thing for animals, but mismatched animals. Like centaur shit. Human and horse. Fish and lion. The lawyer lady was talking about it— real nutty and spacey. I wanted to tell her to shut up and go get laid, but I didn't want a bad Yelp review."

Tempe laughed.

I wanted to play the lottery with whatever numbers Carton wanted.

"How many get fish and lion?" I asked.

"I had four guys over the last few weeks. All tough as nails, creepy guys. This ain't a leisurely, 'I'mma do it when I'm drunk' thing. Whoever gets this ink is pretty connected. I've inked bangers and mobsters and all sorts of cons. This stuff's up there. Find them and maybe you'll find your lawyer lady. Shame she's missing and all that. Seemed decent despite the attitude."

"How much you charge for it?" I asked.

"That's top secret."

"I'd want a refund."

"Tell that to the tall skinny guy with a long beard who paid double last week. Wanted it expedited. Said it was to fuck with other teams in his Serbian soccer league. Intimidation factor times a thousand he said. He got two sharks."

Serbian. Jackpot.

"When do they play?" I asked.

"Monday and Thursday nights in Lincoln Park. He wouldn't shut the fuck up about it, and he tried to stiff me on the fee afterward."

"No bueno," I said.

———

TEMPE TYPED something in her phone, and within seconds we were being chauffeured away by a Bulls fan. I thought the cabbies must be on strike, but Tempe said they were a thing of the past, that everybody toured the city in "Ubers" now. The name sounded like a spoiled recipe of pinto beans, but I went with it. The car had pretzels too.

We rode in silence for a while, Tempe looking at the bright lights from her window and me looking at the back of the chewed-up leather headrest. Cabbies were usually on the ball with interior decor, but I guess the Uber drivers believed in character.

"How did you two meet?" the driver asked.

"Over some deep dish pizza," I said.

Tempe stared daggers at me.

The driver smiled. "There's nothing quite like finding the right person over some of the best cuisine the city has to offer. I met my wife in Little Italy. The best twenty-dollar plate of pasta I ever had."

"Give me carbs or give me death," I said.

The Uber driver smiled and turned up the music in his car. My musical proficiency was putrid; I was more of a beat person. If I liked the beat, I deemed the song a success. If not, then the song was kicked to the curb faster than a kicker who missed a bunch of field goals on Sunday. This driver had chosen well, the beat was perfect, and I found that my ears were slowly acclimating to normal sounds again. I had been out less than a week, but every once in a while a tire screech or car horn startled me. Not even a million books could cure PTSD.

But good music was a start.

Tempe said nothing. I wanted to reach into her skull and see what she was thinking. I knew the silent treatment was a major tool in a woman's arsenal, but I didn't enjoy shades of gray. Certainty was my best friend. Either Tempe enjoyed my company or she didn't. I knew she wanted my clothes off, but I wanted something more.

"I'm going to that soccer game tomorrow," I said.

"Good for you." She looked out her window again. The lights were the same as they were a block ago.

"I'd like it if you joined me."

"Why?"

"To have a second pair of eyes. I don't know my way around that much."

"You grew up here and then got railroaded here. I think you know the place quite well."

"I doubt it."

She sighed, and for the first time I noticed the bags under her eyes. She must have been putting in the hours now that Stevenson was gone.

"I'm up here," she said to the driver.

The car slowed past an intersection and pulled to the right.

Tempe turned to me. "Last chance to split that bottle. Take it or leave it."

"Honesty is the best policy." I tapped my foot to the music some more. It was a different song now, but still a good beat.

"You're crazy," she said.

"Must be all the headshots."

"You won't stop, will you?"

"As long as I'm out, I'm going to find her. And when I do, it'll be hell to pay for whoever messed with her. And I'm finding Henri, too."

Tempe gave me a business card and jotted her personal number on the back. "Get a damned phone and call me tomorrow. Maybe I'll check out the park and bring Henri. He's been staying with me temporarily."

"Swell."

Tempe thanked the driver and got out. The firm must have been good to her, since she walked into a four-star condo building.

"She seems like a keeper," the driver said.

"Depends which way the wind blows," I said.

The driver took me to the shittiest street in the shittiest part of downtown, but the motel looked excellent from the outside. I tried tipping the driver, but he said everything was already paid for.

By cell phone.

I asked him for the best shop in town, and he told me to look online.

9

I woke at ten the next morning. I'd been dreaming of my mom, which happened every other night when I wasn't having nightmares of my cell at Pontiac. She called my name and told me to get up from the canvas. "Get your ass up, champ," she said. "Up! Up! Up! *Now!*" And then I'd get up ready to kick some ass again.

My mom was my biggest cheerleader, but she was also the true champ. Raised by an alcoholic father and a mother who was into boosting cars and snorting cocaine, Mama Patti Gedrin rose out of the abyss and got her degree in English education. Along the way she met an Alaskan crab fisherman named Ronnie Spikes, and thirty-six weeks later I came into the world with my brown hair, brown eyes, and squinty scowl. The crab fisherman didn't come back one day after a sixty-foot wave threw him overboard, so Mom did the parenting thing solo. She was my hero, plain and simple.

Even after I went to Pontiac, she'd visit me every Sunday like clockwork. When the rest of the world had turned their back on me and pretended I didn't exist, Mom was there to tell me the case was thin and the lawyers would figure it all out and to keep my head up. She was my light during the darkest times.

Then she missed a Sunday, and I learned she'd had a fatal stroke.

As much as I wished she could see my second chance in life, I knew it wasn't in the cards. I had to play the ones I was dealt, and that meant fulfilling my purpose. I was never a super religious type, but I had a sense that the ship righted itself in the end and things ended up where they should. My purpose now was to find Stevenson. She was my light after Mom's went out. I had a badass mom coursing through me, a dad I never knew, and a ferocious lawyer who beat the system. Together it was a hellacious combo of indomitable will and spirit that followed me every step of the way.

But I knew that to find Stevenson, I'd have to find myself again. I left the motel and went to the only place that fit the bill: Sal's gym. Twenty years ago I walked in as a rebellious youth trying to beat up the kid who took my lunch money. I walked out with cuffs, a title, and a media circus. Now I planned to go in there and knock off the rust before going to the soccer field at night. I'd call Tempe when I got out, now that I had a phone. I hadn't gone online last night like the driver advised, but I did find the most durable flip phone at one of the local spots. It didn't have any fruit on it, but I was proud to join the masses as a tech hombre.

I dressed and hit the heavy bag first. Unlike the rest of society, the boxing community supported its own. Once a champ, always a champ. As soon as I got into my stance, a few kids asked for a signed picture. I signed, then realized it was a picture of me and Sal right before my first title fight. I smiled and gave the kids an extra pair of wrist wraps.

Sal was no longer the managing partner, but his son still kept the place the way his dad liked it. No headgear. No music.

No water fountains. Hardcore and old school. From time to time Sal would come in and coach up the kids, talking shit every step of the way, but today he was out.

Then I got down to business. I hit the heavy bag, jumped rope, did three hundred pushups, three hundred crunches, seven sets of planks, and went back to the heavy bag. It felt like I never left. Muscle memory is a beautiful thing; it felt like I'd never left. Three hours later, I was spent and could eat a horse. I stretched out.

"Looking fine, champ."

I turned to find Stine standing beside me, admiring the place.

"My jab needs a little more work," I said.

"I've never seen a single woman training in here." Stine was looking at the pictures all over the walls. Buff men in boxing trunks posing with Sal.

"Sal was and is inclusive for all."

Stine laughed and put her hands on her hips. "Any luck with your girl?"

"Nada."

"Why do I feel like I'm being played?"

"Because you are."

I took my gloves off and went to work on my wrist wraps. It was annoying taking off all the layers. It took forever. After a fight, I had a team for that. Now I was flying solo.

Or maybe not. Stine started undoing my wraps.

"You don't have to," I said.

"When was the last time you did your wraps?" she asked.

"When you became a corner woman."

Stine smiled. "My dad won the Golden Gloves in the eighties. I'd follow him around. That's where I picked up my love for the game. It's an art."

Reporters always had a great response for everything, but

Stine seemed genuine—and she undid my wraps in record time.

"I told you to watch out for Kayla Tempe," she said.

"Spying on me must bring you great pleasure," I said.

She frowned. "She's been through the wringer and it shows. Again, watch out for that one."

I didn't know if Stine was exaggerating. Jealousy often set off fires with women.

I said, "She has an attitude, but what lawyer doesn't?"

"She called our office last year complaining about a story we wrote about her DUI client who ran over a family of deer. She called and berated my editor for an hour straight and tried to get him to pull the story. One whole hour. When she was done, she filed a lawsuit, which was dismissed right away. Slow your roll, counselor. That's insane."

"She's doing her job and she's the bad guy?" I laughed at the naïveté.

Stine shook her head. "A woman who acts like that needs to get laid. But I pity the man who marries her."

Getting laid was great, but I agreed with Stine that marriage would be an odd combo. Tempe would object and cite statutes if there were any disputes.

For a moment we watched some kids fooling around on the heavy bag. One kid threw the bag while the others ran into it like bowling pins.

"You'll get your exclusive tonight," I said.

"Excellent. I think it'll be a great story."

Then I let up and told her about the tat and the possible Serbian connection soccer game. She nodded every step of the way, but didn't take notes.

"I bet it's Vegas," she said. "Gertrude defended a Serbian gangster named Vegas a couple years ago. Drug charges. She got a little too close—after court one day somebody saw her holding hands with her client in the elevator. The case dragged and dragged even though all the discovery was complete, and some said it was because she wanted to squeeze the client for more money. Others said it was because the fucking was so good and she was being paid well to prolong the inevitable."

It's hard to figure out your lawyer's sexual habits when you're in a glass interview room, but I had a feeling Stine was on the money. And Tempe wasn't.

"The guy ended up losing at trial. He went down on the drug delivery charges and got sentenced to six years. Gertrude cleverly asked for house arrest at the bond hearing, so Vegas had a bunch of credit before he went in, on top of the day-for-day credit he got upon sentencing. He did about a year."

"I can do a year with my eyes closed." I wouldn't volunteer, but the truth was, having a definite out date did wonders for the psyche compared to the words "death" or "life without parole." "So the scumbag did a year and killed her? That's weak."

"The guy had no record before he went down. Couldn't get a job when he got out. He was pretty young too. His name was all over the papers. Perfect motive to do in the person who couldn't win your case. My runners have been trying to track Vegas down since he got out. Last I heard he was in Paducah, Kentucky, running a gun shop selling everything under the sun. They love their Second Amendment there."

"That's not proof beyond a reasonable doubt," I said.

"He's not in Kentucky anymore. The shop closed down the day before Gertrude went missing."

I watched the kids. They were running into the heavy bag full speed now, and Sal would have a heart attack.

"Vegas is a start," I said. "But there's gotta be people higher up the chain. He's not a shot caller. If he was a jilted lover he would have left a messy trail. He might have done her, but

49

there's no body. Nothing. It doesn't fit. But he could have used people with more skills to get the job done quietly."

"Criminals don't take a body, wrap it up with a little bow, and put their name on it," Stine said.

She was right, but my mind wandered.

"Are you hungry?" I said.

"Yes. Is it a date?"

"No."

"Okay."

I hit the lockers and showered in record time. When I got out, Stine was waiting with a partial frown on her face. I found an upscale diner down the street that had the word "sammich" on the menu. I wolfed down a Denver omelet with pancakes and hash browns on the side, and my stomach didn't protest. Stine had a cinnamon muffin, tea, and a Caesar salad. We talked about fighting and time and love and life. Stine took notes, and this time I let her. She was cool, and a deal was a deal after all. We'd go on camera later. We exchanged numbers, and I went back to the motel. I changed into the same clothes from yesterday and made a mental note that if I came into some cash I'd need to expand my wardrobe again. I didn't have any degrees to elevate my station, but I knew I had more fights in me.

I played around with my phone for a little bit, trying to figure out how to use the internet. I looked over the instruction booklet for ages until I accidentally pressed a button and found it. I came across some more stories about Stevenson, but it was all a rehash of what I already knew. I looked up boxing stats and watched a couple fight highlights. The modern era was all show, no grit.

When I was all done, I pulled out Tempe's business card.

And I dialed her number.

10

Henri ignored the fire hydrant then pissed on two trees before greeting me.

"He's a monster," Tempe said. She was wearing jeans, sneakers, and a nice top. I liked her in non-court attire.

"Keep a loose leash and give him some treats. Positive reinforcement." Henri's pincher ears stood at attention like a class of recruits at roll call. I loved dogs, and had owned a couple before the fall. They were a lot of responsibility, but the reward came back ten-fold. When the state came for me I found a good home for them and made sure they had all their favorite toys.

"He needs a stable home. I don't have much time for him with work. He's super cute though." Tempe rubbed Henri's whiskers, and I did the same. We found a picnic table overlooking a baseball diamond and soccer field. We were at Jonquil Park waiting for the Serbians to show. I wondered whether I should tell Tempe about Vegas, but I decided to let things play out. Sometimes too many eyes on the prize was a bad thing. And I didn't want Tempe running it up the chain at the firm or worse going to CPD's finest to fuck things up.

We stared at the empty baseball field for a while. It was after five, and I had no doubt the field would soon fill up with the after-work crowd.

Tempe broke the silence. "The doctor was answering my questions with his own questions. He lost all credibility in the dep. I'm framing the transcript."

"Sounds like a victory worth celebrating." I smiled, and Tempe returned it. That was the second smile since I'd known her. Things were looking up.

"You had your chance, champ." Tempe rubbed Henri's ears and Henri let out a low whine that said give me more.

If Vegas showed, then I wouldn't hesitate to get my hands dirty. I didn't care how much backup there would be. I looked at the soccer field, and it was filling up with some basketball players. They kicked the ball back and forth to each other for a while and laughed. The basketball court nearby was jam-packed with a full-court game, so the ballers were trying to pass the time till they had next. I analyzed their form for a few minutes.

Then we hit pay dirt.

"That's them," I said. I pointed to the parking lot at the far end of the field. A bunch of imported cars pulled up. Mercedes. Beamers. Audis. Saabs. Europeans tended to drive European cars. My old manager was part Serbian, and he used to dish on his brethren's habits all the time. European cars carried a big badge of pride and success. Muy bueno.

The Serbians piled out of the cars two at a time. Within seconds the b-ballers were overrun and there were eleven new guys on the field, all with tats, but nothing stood out. I knew that getting anything out of them was a long shot. People with things to hide don't cave easily. Criminals especially. They refused to snitch and would rather take things to the grave. It was a matter of self-preservation. But if the opportunity presented itself, I'd take my shot. I never quit. In the ring I'd walk my opponents down, always trying to score the big knockout. The fans loved it, but Sal and the rest of the team had coronary episodes every time since I exposed myself too much. Going for big-time knockouts meant possibly getting big-time knockouts in return. But that's how I rolled. While most boxers were built up by suave promoters who gave them undefeated records over shitty opponents, I wanted to fight anybody and everybody. I didn't care about the loss column.

So Vegas was done.

Tempe yawned. "Other than interfering with an ongoing police investigation, are you contributing to society in any other way?"

"I'm currently seeking employment that satisfies both body and mind."

"We're hiring investigators at the firm. I think you'd fit in somewhere."

Timing is everything sometimes. I was down to my last cents because of the damned cell phone and was going to persuade the motel keeper to have me on staff till I booked a fight. "I don't have a resume."

"We all know your resume. The partners wouldn't shut up about you yesterday. They think having a fighter, literally *and* figuratively would do wonders for the company morale."

"And bring in more business." I knew the score. Bring in an ex-celebrity nutcase who was accused of murder, and the floodgates open. Clients loved famous lawyers, and they pay up for it. But I was no slouch. I could drive a hard bargain any day of the week.

"I need hourly plus expenses, and I need an advance. For security reasons."

"The CTE must be doing a number on you," Tempe said.

She smirked and went back to Henri. He was chewing some of the picnic table.

"What's the dress code?"

"Business casual for you. Business for me."

"Cool."

We worked out a deal. Tempe said the hourly and expenses were part of the normal course of business, but she'd have to work on the advance. I shook her hand and was hired. But I knew better than that. Until I signed on the dotted line nothing was official and my cash was in limbo.

The Serbians did some stretches and picked teams. They took the game really seriously, because they started by doing some passing drills. We sat in silence for a while. For most humans silence is awkward; they always try to fill the void with something quirky or unintelligible. For me, silence is golden. It allows me to calm my mind and get more in tune with my body.

My heart rate slowed, and I took in everything around me. I became one with nature.

Then somebody blew a whistle and the game started.

The Serbians played five on five with one in goal. After a couple minutes, some stragglers came and it was seven on seven, then eight on eight. The Serbians kicked a decent ball and had great footwork. They hustled and argued like the pros. At one point, the ball flew toward the picnic table, Henri slobbered on it, and Tempe threw it back.

"You're a natural," I said.

She punched me in the shoulder, and I wanted more. Fact. Physical contact was the first step to deeper intimacy.

"Wow," she said. She pointed to the parking lot, and I clenched my fists. "We got played."

A new player had arrived. It wasn't Vegas, but it was somebody who deserved to get pummeled just as much.

I took out my phone.

"Is that a Jitterbug?" Tempe said.

I had no idea what the hell she was talking about.

She pointed to my phone. "That's for senior citizens."

"I got a great deal."

I pressed a button on the phone and snapped a couple pictures.

"Impressive," Tempe said.

I followed my target from midfield to the goal. There were two scenarios. Either he would come over and greet us and play nice, or he would make things difficult. I hoped for the latter.

He shook hands with the other Serbians on the field, did some quick stretches, then took someone's place in goal.

"Can Henri bite on cue?" I said.

"He can poop on cue," Tempe said.

"Okay."

The target stopped a couple testy shots and gained confidence. Things went on like that for a good seven minutes. Nothing could get past him.

And then he saw me.

I smiled.

The punk rocker kid from Fat Tony's ran for his life.

11

But I was faster.

And Henri was even faster.

Within ten strides I was even with the kid. Henri growled and nipped at the kid's heels. On the eleventh stride, I clotheslined the kid and knocked the wind out of him. I knew what would happen next—the rest of the Serbians would want retribution after their brains registered what was happening. Henri couldn't take all of them out, and now he was distracted with a tree branch.

I quickly did the count. Sixteen of them. Half would run away or freeze up. Three would be clumsy and uncoordinated. Two would be too fat to tie their shoelaces.

That left three.

Three would be a handful.

I got the numbers right. Three courageous ones were on me faster than I could say hello. Luckily for me, I had experienced a lifetime of being bum-rushed. In the ring from crazed fans and on the inside when trying to convince the pod to watch the cooking channel. The key was to keep your distance and always make the first move.

I sidestepped Serbian number one and elbowed Serbian two in the solar plexus. Serbian three threw a weak right, and I slipped it and threw a solid left hook, knocking the guy into next week.

Two left.

I shuffled backward to keep my eyes on both targets. They had dilated pupils and sweaty foreheads—the universal signs of fear. I smiled, and number one tried to tackle me. I swatted his head down with my fist, then stepped on his hand. We weren't playing by the Nevada Athletic Commission rules, and I felt totally free. While the first dude writhed in pain, the second tried to finish the job. Pride cometh before the fall. He pulled a small knife out of his pocket and lunged at me.

I had experience with knives too.

I twisted the guy's hand and in one fluid motion flipped the knife on him, slicing his forearm. I squeezed the knife handle like I was going in for another slice and said, "Are you done?"

He ran away.

Serbian one did too.

Serbian three would have done the same, but he was still counting sheep. That left the kid. And me. And Henri, who was rolling on his back, loving life.

The kid staggered back to his feet, holding his throat. Tempe caught up to us as I asked him, "Where's Vegas?"

The kid was shaking. "What the hell are you talking about, dude?"

"Cut the bullshit. You were hanging on Fat Tony's every word. He swatted you away like a water bug."

The kid brushed some dirt off his shirt and looked toward the parking lot. "You don't know anything."

"Enlighten us."

"No," the kid said.

"A body shot or a head shot?" I said.

The kid looked at Tempe, then at me, then at the Serbian who was having a horrible day, then at Henri. Finally he took a deep breath and faced me square. "I'm going into a box if I tell you."

"If nobody saw it, then it didn't happen," I said.

The kid's eyes left mine and held Tempe's. "They have eyes and ears everywhere. The brotherhood never stops. Blood in, blood out."

"Serbian mob," I said. I left Stine out of it.

The kid nodded. "I'm a runner. They always paid better than that asshole Fat Tony. They whistle, I whistle back. They say jump, I say how high. They bailed me out of jail a lot, and I owe them my life. These eyes have been through hell and back. But you cross 'em, you cross 'em. There's no takebacks."

I looked around the field to see if any Serbians found their courage again. The field was a ghost town. But the play area wasn't. A group of parents were looking in my direction, phones in hand.

Shit.

CPD's finest were coming.

"Did Vegas do her in?" I said.

"Who?" the kid asked.

"Gertrude Stevenson."

The kid shook his head. "I don't know specifics, dude. I play soccer with them, I drink with them sometimes, and I wait for a call from the big boss. It's as simple as that. And I got this stupid-ass tattoo." He rolled up his shirt and showed the horrid shark.

"Your nose ring twitches when you lie," Tempe said.

The kid laughed.

I smiled. I'd been in Tempe's orbit barely twenty-four hours, and had already come to appreciate her wit and charm.

I brushed some more grass off the kid's shirt. "Hundred bucks tells me you know where Vegas is hiding."

"Wrong man."

Then Serbian number three got up. I gave him a quick uppercut, and the man just couldn't catch a break. Any air of confidence the kid had gained quickly vanished.

I stretched my neck a few times, not taking my eyes off him.

The kid looked around the field for his saving grace. He didn't find it. He was toast.

After twenty seconds of silence, the kid spoke in a low voice. "Vegas is a hit man for the boss. You don't cross Vegas. He keeps records."

Before I could ask him who the boss was, Tempe said, "They're coming."

Police sirens blared in the distance.

No way in hell I was going back to jail.

Before I could tell Tempe the plan, she took off with Henri. I heard screaming in the distance.

And I turned on the jets.

12

I hung a right on the corner, then a quick left. I found a one-way zigzag street and hid behind a dilapidated sedan that had run out of style thirty years ago. The sirens got louder, but the screaming was gone. Which didn't mean shit, because now there were choppers and dogs even bigger than Henri who could find me in a heartbeat.

I looked out from behind the sedan and saw a cop sprinting past the corner. He'd bring the cavalry in no time once somebody called in the big suspicious dude looking like a booster. I scanned left and right for an opening.

Bingo. An abandoned lot with a small fence. No more than twenty steps away. A bus shelter on the other side. Perfecto. I waited a minute to see if there were any reinforcements, then I went for it.

My track record with fences was an even five hundred. I hadn't jumped a fence since high school, and it showed. I banged my knee on the way up, but I got over, ran to the bus shelter, and admired the Selena Gomez fragrance ad. I didn't know who she was, but the fragrance seemed fancy and she seemed happy to call it her own. I looked at the bus schedule and realized that nothing was coming anytime soon. I needed an out, quickly. Calling Tempe was out of the question; she was with Henri, and besides, there was no way she'd risk getting caught. Granted, she'd probably lawyer her way out of it, but she wouldn't put herself in that position if she could avoid it.

I racked my brain and came up with the only person who could get the job done. And the only other person whose number I had in my phone.

Stine.

I called her. Seven minutes later she pulled up in a news van. I hopped in back where all the equipment was.

She looked back at me. "When I said I'd help you out, I didn't mean aiding and abetting."

"Innocent till proven guilty."

"You're lucky nobody in the park ID'd you. Right now they're looking for a white male, tall with a blue shirt. I know a million people who fit that. Open that bag. There's a red shirt in there. You're on your own with the bottoms."

I changed into the red shirt and fixed my hair. My jeans were a dime a dozen, so I felt comfortable keeping them. I stayed low in back as Stine crossed each intersection.

Then she called me out.

"There's tints. I take it this fiasco tonight happened with your little girlfriend Ms. Tempe?"

"That's a fallacious label, but yes she was present and so was Henri."

"I've been looking for Henri," Stine said. "He'd add a little more puff to the piece. A little more warmth."

"You'll get an exclusive with Henri standing on my head if you get me the hell outta here," I said. I didn't know where, but the farther away from the sirens, the better.

"Did your little escapade yield anything fruitful?" Stine asked.

"The kid from Fat Tony's was there. And I kicked his ass a little bit."

"Great. Add battery to your crime spree."

"Self-defense. I can beat that case any day of the week."

Stine laughed. "I like how you're so brazen. Give me more of that on camera." She picked up speed and we found the highway.

"The kid claimed Vegas is a hit man."

"No surprise," Stine said. "He closed the gun shop and moonlights as a thug. Works for some crime syndicate probably and gets away with everything under the sun. I know life's not a movie, but in this case it probably is."

"His boss has to be international. No way he's chilling around Chicago ordering his minions to get him strawberry lattes. I bet it's London or Prague. Fancy. Where else would the gang stay? Vegas gets the call from out east and makes the family proud."

"If we were talking about Italians and Irish, I'd agree with you. The real muscle's back home. But when Serbians migrated to America the majority settled in Chicago. It's a heavy, authentic European enclave. We did a bunch of pieces on their culture and cuisine. They love this city and their mark is all over it. Vegas could be walking among us laughing at our stupidity."

"Why would the big boss care about a bullshit drug case? He's got bigger fish to fry, unless they hired Stevenson for a murder that she botched. But I doubt it. Stevenson kicked ass on every case."

"She kicked ass, but even the greats go down. When you deal in the criminal world, things never quite go your way. It's only a matter of time before the help becomes the hunted.

Gotti's lawyer was talking smart and beating cases, but then they caught the Teflon Don trying to put a hit out on him in the end."

"They kicked him off the case, that's why," I said. My cellies wouldn't shut up about it for a week straight when it went down.

"Bottom line, lawyers and clients don't always make for a happy marriage. There's more to Gertrude than meets the eye. Just like there's more to you, and to me. Open your eyes. You want something more concrete, you need to see her files. But that'd be another crime on your spree. Theft of legal documents."

"Not one bit," I said. I told Stine that I'd been hired as an investigator.

"*Definitely* watch out for Kayla now," Stine said. "She's luring you in with a job and will break your heart in the end. Have you slept with her yet? Don't. She'll have you wrapped around her finger like a yo-yo."

I tried not to laugh, but I knew she was right. If Tempe and I hit the sheets, things would never be the same again. That's how it always went. One party was happy, and the other less so. Like two crooked railroad tracks that never quite met up.

The van took an exit off the highway and turned left on a winding road that passed under a couple viaducts. "We'll go back to my place. You can spend the night, but first thing in the morning you'll freshen up and we'll do the exclusive. Better to have a live shot early in the morning so we make the news cycle. Every network will follow our lead. We'll go over some talking points."

"Sounds like a plan."

Stine stopped at another intersection, and I heard rubber ripping pavement. I lied when I said I was getting used to loud noises. I recoiled in my seat, and the bullets came. The van was lit up. Then the rubber screeched and tore away.

I took my hands from over my head and crawled past the glass littered all over the floor.

Stine wouldn't get her exclusive.

She was slumped over the wheel in a pool of blood.

13

I managed to get a glimpse of the car screeching away. On a scale of 1 to 10, the glimpse was a 0.5. Black SUV. Tints. Blurry out-of-state plates. Which was all meaningless and made for a big-ass headache if I was ever asked to give a statement. When I was completely done sweating buckets I went around to the driver's side. Even though I knew already, I checked for Stine's pulse.

Nada.

Whoever did this had made sure it was a one-time deal. Stine had multiple bullet wounds.

Life in the ring had made me numb to blood. Noses. Lips. Ears. Mouths. Knuckles. Giving and receiving. But this time was different. No amount of training could prepare me for this. As the blood pooled in Stine's seat and dripped onto the floorboards, the color slowly drained from her face. She went from a sparkly reporter to an ashen mass of flesh. I'd go to the grave knowing exactly how body decomposition worked.

I looked around. The street was deserted. I realized that I was now wrapped up in two murders. The killer, or killers, had planned it perfectly. Follow the van to the middle of nowhere, take out the target, and leave a witness behind with so much baggage that he'd be suspected of doing it. Add the park incident from earlier, and I was easily suspect numero uno. And with no alibi I was finished. I needed an out. A plan. And a damned good one.

I closed my eyes, but nothing came. Then I remembered *Law & Order*. My DNA was all over the place. Prints too.

I went back to Stine's body, rifled through her bag, and came away with a key, a wallet, and a pen. The wallet would get me to Stine's place, the key would get me through the door, and the pen would serve as a weapon. I searched the rest of the van in two minutes. I checked the equipment in back for anything useful, but came up empty. I grabbed a rag from behind the passenger seat and wiped down everything I could possibly have come into contact with. Which was basically every damned surface. I did a shitty job and missed a bunch of spots, but then I did a second pass and got every last inch of me outta there.

I knew that when the detectives came out for this one they'd be taking orders directly from the mayor. *Find the scum who killed one of our very own public servants.* They'd ransack the van a million different ways to find a profile. An innocent man should have nothing to worry about, but I knew better. When all leads were exhausted, somebody would play patsy.

I closed my eyes and took a deep breath. Idaho looked damned good right about now.

I looked at Stine one last time. My purpose was two-fold now. Find Stevenson, and find the piece of shit who did this. I promised Stine I wouldn't let up, and I left the van in the dead of night on a deserted street in the middle of nowhere. I had no idea where I was going, but I figured I'd find my way eventually.

I passed a park that made Jonquil look like Goliath, then an ice cream shop, a rustic library, and an old-school movie theater. When I found a gas station with a bathroom, I went to work.

The red shirt Stine gave me did a nice job blending in with blood, but a horrible job absorbing it. Underneath, my body looked like a pack of wolves had found their new toy. I took the shirt off and ran it under the faucet. The basin filled, and for a moment I thought it was wine. I fixed my hair and threw water in my face. My eyes couldn't believe the set on the other side of the mirror. I craned my neck left and right looking for any more remnants of blood. I checked my teeth too.

Then the clerk knocked on the door. "Hello! Customers only!"

He kept knocking, and I kept blow-drying the hell out of the shirt. But my faith in the power of the gas station dryer was stupid. I flipped the shirt over and wrung it out and twisted it every which way, but it was no use. It wasn't getting dry.

I tossed the shirt in the bag and, taking a gamble, put the blue shirt back on. A clerk working the night shift wasn't going to be keeping tabs on the local blotter from earlier. He didn't care what was going on around him so long as customers paid for their gas and Twinkies and went about their merry way.

I stepped outside.

"Asshole," the clerk said. "I see you rummaging around here again and I'm calling the police."

"Lo Siento," I said. I asked him where my amazing motel was and the clerk pointed me in the right direction. As I walked away, I held the bag over my right shoulder thinking it would hide me better.

The night was cool and the city lights peeked out of hiding with each step. Along the way I encountered squirrels, rabbits, one fox, one rat, but no cops. Twelve minutes later I crossed an intersection and found the motel parking lot. Much had changed since the morning. The "Vacancies, Free Cable" sign was missing one bulb, jazz music was playing, and the lot was filled with station wagons and bumper stickers.

I took the stairs to my second-floor room.

Tempe was waiting outside.

Henri was gone.

14

"You're okay," Tempe said.

She hugged me, and I was in Heaven. She smelled like lilacs and peppermint. The seconds ticked away and we were like two high schoolers greeting each other after summer break. We would have stayed like that for a while if it wasn't for the drunk next door. A glass bottle broke, followed by another one.

Tempe pulled away first.

I opened the door and she came in. My place wasn't the Ritz, but I'd made sure to stock the mini-fridge with water bottles and grapes. I handed a bottle to Tempe and tossed my bag on the bed.

Tempe stared at me for a moment then took a swig. She did it elegantly and with poise. My swig was swift and violent.

"You're lucky I'm a lawyer," she said.

"Lawyers are shysters," I said.

"When the officers caught me, I was ready."

"Did you release Henri on them?"

"No."

"Where is he?"

"Back home."

"Did you feed him?"

"Yeah."

I could have used the little guy right about now. Dogs were not only man's best friend, they were man's best therapy. If Henri were here he would get a belly rub and I would try and get over the fact that I was almost butchered in a news van. Henri would listen to the whole story and would get treats for his empathy.

Tempe put her water bottle down and found a mirror to the right of the TV. Part elixir and part kryptonite, the mirror had a complicated history with the female sex. Tempe turned to one side and checked herself out. Then she turned to the other side and checked herself out. She stood there for a while, moving left, right, front, back. Fast. Slow. She shook her head at times and smiled at others. She was sending me a message that I appreciated, but wasn't in the mood for given the circumstances.

Tempe said, "I told them it was all a big misunderstanding. The kid was there too. They caught up with him in a heartbeat."

"That punk had it coming."

"He was tongue-tied and kept looking back toward the parking lot. I told them there was too much testosterone on the field and nobody wanted to take things any further. A couple witnesses said their kids were scarred for life, but I flashed my bar card and ran my mouth some more, and that's all she wrote."

"Excellent. She who gets the last breath usually wins. Where did the kid go?"

"I have no idea. The minute the cops wrapped up, he was

gone. Maybe he hopped in a Beamer and called it a day. Or maybe he's a ghost."

"I need to find the boss and introduce myself." The kid was full of shit on a lot of things, but when he brought up the boss I knew he was telling the truth. The eyes never lied when the adrenaline was pumping and cortisol was filling the body. The kid was the low man on the totem pole, and there were bigger and badder fish to fry. I was hungry and wanted the people that had the answers to the crucial questions at the crucial times. And I'd get them, come hell or high water. Find the boss, and Vegas would follow.

"You need to get up early tomorrow," Tempe said. "Work starts at eight." She smiled and went back to her water bottle.

My head was throbbing, but I ignored it. The body could take a lot of wear and tear, but eventually it would fight back. I didn't want to work just yet, but I really needed to get back on my feet, and sometimes Benjamins were the best medicine.

"How 'bout that advance?" I said.

"Show up on time and I'll take care of the rest. You're in good hands with all the suits."

"Can't wait."

Tempe picked up an ashtray and tossed it over in her hands like it was a stress ball. It went like that for a couple minutes before she got bored.

"I can't have you getting cancer," she said. "You should get the patch."

"I don't smoke," I said.

Tempe said nothing.

I turned on the TV and flipped to a basketball game. The Bulls weren't playing, but the Lakers were.

"What's in the bag?" Tempe asked.

I shrugged. "A change of clothes."

Certain things were best left unsaid. Especially when it

meant breathing fresh air and having my own toothbrush. Plead the fifth. DTA. Don't. Trust. Anybody. Tempe was a lawyer and lawyers knew these things, but she wasn't *my* lawyer. Maybe it was Stine in my ear, or maybe it was my hubris, but Tempe would get the full scoop when *I* wanted to give it. And now that we were coworkers, lunch table gossip was real.

She sat on the edge of the bed and watched some of the game. She leaned back at one point and her hand grazed mine. I played dead.

The Lakers were up three in the final seconds. Then the visiting team called a timeout when they didn't have one, which resulted in a technical foul. The Lakers iced the game with a free throw, and the fans got commemorative yellow t-shirts.

"That was a technicality," Tempe said.

"Rules are rules," I said.

"That's no fun."

"Technicalities are the great equalizer."

Tempe got up from the bed and went back to the mirror. She did one last twirl and craned her neck, then looked back at me. "I'm going out on a limb for you. Don't fuck this up. Wear something nice tomorrow."

And just like that, Tempe was gone. I pictured myself in boxing trunks and a hoodie making a grand entrance into the firm. I smiled, then I went back down the stairs to the motel keeper. Nobody was on duty, so I rang the bell. I heard rustling in back, then the keeper showed his face. He was wearing an Attitude Era shirt.

"We have no more vacancies," the keeper said. He had one eye open and one eye half open.

"Where's the lost and found?" I said.

He eyed me like I had the plague, then pulled a cardboard

box from under the desk. "Not many treasures left I suppose." He put the box on the counter and opened the flaps.

He was right. Aside from a soccer ball, a lanyard, and a broken sandal, there wasn't much to be proud of. I shook the box to see if any animals would come out and greet me.

Nada.

But then I hit the jackpot. Nestled deep in the corner, under the sandal and scrunched up in a little ball, was a light-pink dress shirt.

"That one," I said.

The keeper pulled it out, but the shirt stayed scrunched up. "This one's been here since Valentine's Day. Top-of-the-line cotton though."

He handed me the shirt, and I scrutinized it better than one of my own fight films. This was the best I could do. The shops were closed now, and wouldn't open in time to get anything on credit in the morning. I asked the keeper how much I owed, but he waved me off and went back to his bed in back.

I passed the stairs to my room and went straight to the laundry. I washed the shirt three times with three spare quarters I found by the machine. When I finally got back to my room, the postgame show was over.

The news was on.

And Stine's body had already been found by CPD.

15

I got four and a half hours of sleep and woke up feeling like a freight train had said hello and goodbye. I showered and ate a light breakfast. Bagel and a banana. My stomach appreciated the variety. I checked the TV on Stine's death; the consensus was multiple shooters, serious marksmen. I wholeheartedly agreed.

I checked the clock and realized I needed to get moving. I made a pact with myself in high school that I'd never be late for work. From my days as a cart pusher at the local grocery to my days in training camp, I respected the clock and the institutions that swore by it. The early bird gets the worm. Always. The early bird also had time to gather his thoughts and focus on the tasks at hand. Maximum efficiency. Maximum concentration. Maximum reward. I wasn't breaking the habit now.

I showed up for my first day of work at 7:42. The firm was a ghost town. Either the lawyers went straight to court in the morning or the madness started once they had two pots of Joe. I sat in the same plush chair and analyzed the same artwork. There wasn't a secretary telling me to wait this time, but I still didn't think it was appropriate to barge into the offices like I owned the place. Lawyers were anal about details. I needed my advance, and I needed them to think I wasn't a client trying to rob the place. Once a con, always a con. The stigma followed me like a skunk's perfume.

Luckily, my pink dress shirt traveled well. From the hands of an unknown human to a lonely box to the chest of a champ, the fabric screamed sophistication and success. Add my pressed jeans, clean Chelsea boots, and gray socks, and I was in business. I hoped the moxie would rub off on some of the partners and they would feel emboldened to open their coffers. As much as I appreciated the concept of contributing to a large organization, an employee's gotta eat first.

I picked up a magazine, but was more concerned about whether Tempe would approve of my ensemble. I pictured her eyeing me up and down then making a bunch of sarcastic comments about my color combos. Every time she dissed me I was even more turned on. My mind said to keep playing sleuth and find all the bad hombres who did in Stevenson and Stine, but my heart said to follow Tempe. I enjoyed being around her, and when I wasn't trying to stay out of jail I found myself constantly wondering where I stood with her. I was like a kid on the playground getting butterflies when a girl asked me to play kickball. I knew it was weird to feel a connection with someone after knowing them only two days, but deep down it felt right. On the inside I'd often get fan mail from many admirers, but I was deprived of human contact and longed for something meaningful and stable. Maybe Tempe was the one. The pizza was excellent. The hand-holding sublime. The hug was muy bueno. She was hot and cold and her emotions swung faster than Niagara Falls. But she was real, and she called me out on my shit. Champ or not.

I flipped through the magazine and found a story on crazed

paparazzi. I didn't get more than a paragraph in before Tempe said, "That look is tragic."

She was standing next to the reception desk with her hands on her hips again. She wore a tight blue pantsuit, brown pumps, and a white necklace. I tried to keep my eyes above shoulder level.

She motioned for me to follow, then led me past the conference room from the other day, past a break room, past the bathrooms, and to a small office with half a window view of other tall buildings in the city. A concrete jungle.

"What size jacket are you?" she asked. She opened up a closet to the right of her desk and pulled out some hangers.

"Forty long," I said.

"Too bad. I've got a thirty-six long and a thirty-eight regular. Squeeze those abs into the thirty-eight."

I smiled, and Tempe seemed to return it, but I couldn't tell because she was pulling a bunch of ties out. She tossed some paisleys, checks, and stripes on the desk. A rainbow of epic proportions.

"You keep all your exes' stuff in that closet?" I said.

"Only the ones I killed." She stared me down for a moment, then all the pearly whites came out. "They're for our forgetful clients who have jury trials. Dress to impress."

I did as I was told; I squeezed into the thirty-eight and went with one of the paisley ties. It was more professional, but still seemed out of whack. I never looked good in suits. Still, if the partners were cutting the checks I'd suck it up and enjoy every minute of it. I'd walk the runway, for Christ's sake.

"Come here," Tempe said. She took my hand and pulled me close. We were inches apart. My forehead was getting warm and my elbows too.

She fixed my tie. "Single Windsor. Don't wanna seem too eager. Partners come into the conference room right at eight for the daily agenda. You'll be one of the talking points. Don't do or say anything stupid or juvenile."

"I need access to all the files," I said.

"That's not first-day material."

"Vegas can't get away with this. And the boss too."

"Easy, detective. You have two names and nothing else. You're fucked. After you're vetted by the partners I'll *think* about showing you the stash."

"Thanks, Mom." I rolled my eyes.

She cinched my tie and fixed the lapels of my jacket. Then she ran her hands down my chest real slow, teasing me, tapped my shoulder blades, and went to her desk. As she fixed her makeup with a little mirror, I couldn't take it anymore.

"How many exes do you have?" I asked. "Cumulatively from the last twelve years?"

"It's 7:59. Let's go."

She walked me to the conference room and showed me a seat in back. The room was filled with suits, except one person in front.

And I knew the guy.

16

Quinton Murdock held the record for biggest bench press on the Pontiac prison yard. At five-eight and barely over two hundred pounds, his feat was impressive. Cons of all stripes would cheer him on as he put plate after plate on the bar and kicked ass. I spotted him once, and Murdock gave me the best piece of advice I ever got on the inside.

"Nobody finna do shit if you hard inside an' out. They be workers and you be the boss. Never back down from nobody."

I took the advice to heart and didn't let anybody break me. Physically I was already untouchable. I knew nobody could throw down with me. When it was one on one with fists and knuckles and arms and legs, I took everybody to school. But mentally I had to go twelve rounds every second of every day. Breathing in the musty air. Staring at the gray slabs of concrete till my eyes bled. Listening to the shanks sharpening at night.

I spotted Murdock a few more times on the yard, and we talked about family and friends and my fights. He always wanted to know if the scores were fixed and the ring girls were married. Then one day he wasn't on the yard and I learned he'd gotten a pardon from the governor. I never got the chance to thank him.

Until now.

He was sitting all the way in front, right next to a suit with a stylish pen and legal pad. I figured he was one of the partners, and I was right.

"All right, let's get started," the suit said. "A couple things on the agenda this morning. First off, I want to thank everybody for putting on a brave face and doing great work with the clients while Gertrude is still out there. It hasn't been easy, but it's a testament to the strength and professionalism of this team. We'll keep fighting the good fight and keep doing great work by our clients. I know we all want her here kicking ass with us, but it's not meant to be right now. If we hear any updates, we'll let you know."

Some of the suits shook their heads and murmured around the room as the partner picked up steam.

"Now, some comings and goings. Mort is retiring in a few weeks and we're going to throw him a party worthy of his thirty years of service. Pitch in by the end of the week. As for the newbies—I'm sure you've noticed them milling around the office—I'd like to start by introducing Quinton Murdock, who joined us last week. Quinton was accused of holding up a 7-Eleven when he was eighteen. The clerk didn't ID him, the surveillance footage was blurry, his lawyer slept through half the trial, and he went downstate for a long time. The appeals court didn't care, and when the state wouldn't do the right thing in the interest of justice, luckily the governor did. Quinton got pardoned and has been sharing his story around the country ever since. We're lucky to have him here as an investigator. He's doing some special projects right now, but soon enough he'll be working with the rest of the attorneys."

There was a round of applause, and Murdock smiled.

I slinked down in my chair, but it was futile.

"Now, we won't have just one high-profile investigator, we'll have two. You sports nuts might know him already; he's been hanging around here the last couple days. Lance Gedrin won the heavyweight boxing title fifteen years ago. When he came to town to prep for another title defense, he partied with some friends, went to crash with his trainer, and found himself walked right out of the gym in cuffs, accused of murder. He was sent downstate for an even longer time than Quinton, but Gertrude believed in his innocence from day one, and her hard work paid off—she got his conviction vacated last week. The state is still playing games with the case, but we're confident that they'll do the right thing and see what every justice-oriented person sees. He's one-hundred-percent innocent and was railroaded. Lance will also be doing some special projects initially, then he'll be helping out with the rest of your cases. He'll do great things here."

The crowd was rougher with me. No ovation. They whispered things and had weird looks on their faces. I didn't expect any high-fives, but I at least expected an ID and notepad. I got neither. Apparently an alleged murderer wasn't as cool as an alleged robber. I sat up in my chair and forced a smile that nobody returned. Then Tempe started clapping and the rest of the suits mechanically followed. My advance was on thin ice.

Two other partners added some meaningless filler, and that was it—the meeting was adjourned. Some stayed and grabbed coffee. Some ran out with their cell phones in their ears. Some attacked the breakfast spread at the front. My focus was on the one blueberry muffin left, but before I could get to it, Tempe grabbed my arm and introduced me to some of the big wigs. I shook hands and gave a bunch of platitudes. I smiled and asked the right questions at the right moments. I forgot all their names, but I nodded at every word and laughed at every joke. I was a natural. The mingling lasted a few minutes, and when it was all over the muffin was gone. The partners cleared the room, and Murdock found me.

He said, "My brotha I see you landed on your feet."

"Thanks to you, man." We hugged and stood there lost in time, marveling at how small a world we lived in. From the inside to the outside. Both our lives were destroyed in a court-room, and now we were essentially working in a courtroom. Working for lawyers, having both been screwed by more than our fair share of lawyers. Life was a riot, and we were the bit players.

"Shame 'bout your lawyer," Murdock said. "To beat their asses on appeal is damned good. I had somebody like that from the beginning, I wouldn't need to kiss no governor's ass. I gotta do luncheons now."

"He can't undo the pardon, man. You're free and clear to take the Olympia. I'm still hanging with my case. But I'm gonna find Stevenson."

Murdock flexed his biceps like he was on the yard. I did the same. That was how we rolled. "Keep the faith, brotha. You look hard enough, you can do anything."

"What are the suits making you work on?" I asked.

"They sayin' 'special projects' but ain't nothing special about a client picking up a DUI case and saying ain't the driver. His cousin was. Cousin is hiding from me."

"Start with one plate and work your way up. Keep the faith and you'll be running things here like you were there."

Murdock smiled and took out his phone. "What are your digits? You need anything hit me up."

I pulled out my phone and exchanged numbers with Murdock. Then he winked, tipped his imaginary cap, and was gone.

Now that the suits had cleared the room I could see the lake again. It was even more beautiful than the last time I saw it. I wanted to run a few miles along the path and soak it all in.

Tempe came up behind me. "We have a problem."

I kept staring at the lake. I could have done so all day and been a happy camper. But I was on the clock.

17

Tempe's secretary wheeled in ten banker boxes on a dolly, and Tempe directed her to place the files on the now deserted conference table.

"These are all her open files," Tempe said. "If you want the closed files, we have an outside company that comes in and stores them offsite. Only one partner has the key, and he's in Tahiti for a month. Gertrude had the other key."

I grabbed an empty glass and filled it with water from a pitcher. Dehydration made me hangry, so I needed to up my intake of H_2O.

"I want the thuggish files," I said. "No traffic tickets or disorderly conduct bullshit. Vegas is a repeat customer, and he's probably no angel."

The secretary shook her head and walked out.

Tempe said, "Way to ingratiate yourself with the rest of the staff. I'm sure she'll be eager to peruse the files with you any day of the week."

"I'll get her flowers. Some of those real pink ones in a nice bouquet."

Tempe laughed. "You'll need a whole truck to get back in the game with her. Her husband ditched her for an aspiring actress last year and she'll never live it down." She opened up one of the banker boxes, pulled out some files, and dropped them on the table. "Start with Edgar or Rockens. They had some fishy ties I think, but Gertrude liked to work up the files solo. She brought us underlings in at the end to spell-check and do all the writing. Still, if there were any red flags we would have noticed it, unless we were too pissed and overworked to give a shit."

"Partners get the glory and the minions get the half-baked crazy-ass story. High six figures to babysit and listen to the quacks sounds about right."

I started with the Edgar file. Twisted paperclips and torn yellow half sheets lined the inside. A dry, brown mixture caked some of the dog-eared corners. As I leafed through the pages I hoped it was coffee.

From the looks of it, Edgar liked obtaining unauthorized control over Apple products. Unlike Murdock, Edgar's alleged misdeeds took place on the street, not a convenience store. Two tourists were stuck up by Buckingham fountain and had their iPhones and Airpods taken. Edgar was identified in a photo lineup and charged with armed robbery.

I shook my head and wondered once again why someone would name electronics after a fruit. I still had a lot to learn on the outside, but I'd keep trying. Maybe I'd finally figure out the tweets and the birds and all that.

I said, "How much are iPhones?"

Tempe said, "More than you get every month."

"Where's my advance?"

"If you're a good boy you'll get it soon enough."

I smiled. "I'll be as good as you want me to be."

I didn't care if the check was five hundred bucks or five hundred cents. Things were trending upward.

I flipped through some more pages of the Edgar file hoping to find a gang connection or mob connection. Maybe that would get me closer to Vegas. Which would get me one step closer to the boss. One pebble at a time and before long there'd be a solid path to the prize. The trail was still warm.

I didn't find the smoking gun in the file, but I found the photo lineup. Edgar had tats all over his neck and face, while the other guys in the photos looked like clean-cut choir boys. This pissed me off, and it must have pissed off Stevenson too because she'd written "suggestive lineup" in red ink.

"Mr. Edgar needs to steal a different fruit next time."

Tempe didn't get my joke at first, then it sunk in. She shook her head, touched my right shoulder, and placed the Rockens file in front of me. I was pleased, but I wasn't that easy.

"How long are you gonna babysit me for?" I said. I furrowed my brows like a bulldog and pretended I had influenza. But really Tempe could babysit me day and night if she wanted. It'd be fun.

"Would you like that?" she said. "Seems like you could use help organizing. You're a total noob." She flashed a wide smile and moved her chair a little closer. That made double-digit smiles since I'd met her. I counted them the way I counted new whiteheads on my skin. Which was with extreme precision and reflection. Smiles were magnificent.

Rockens's file was cleaner inside and out, but the theme was still larceny. Taking an HDTV out of Walmart. It was a felony case because of the price of the TV. The state refused to consider Black Friday pricing in its analysis. I pored through the discovery for any Serbian- sounding name or any mention of an organization or club. Any link could make a difference. I had no idea what kind, but I figured it would hit me in the face

GREG GOUNTANIS

at the right time. Give me enough time to figure it out and I'd
be the king.

On the inside I had plenty of hours to hone my craft, so I
dominated the puzzle game. Rubik's cube, jigsaw puzzle,
nobody could stop me. And I wasn't about to cede my crown to
anybody on the outside.

I flipped through some more pages and wondered if Stine
was wrong about the Vegas-Stevenson romance. I couldn't
picture Stevenson stooping so low to get laid by a client. But I
wasn't going to rule it out until I had something concrete.

"What if the kid was bullshitting us the whole time?"
Tempe said. She tossed another file on the pile that I'd created
on the desk.

"The kid was playing us from the jump but pissing his
pants at the end. Fear makes things crystal clear. The eyes don't
lie. Vegas is real and the boss too. We have to find these assholes
before it's too late. Every second counts."

Tempe said nothing, and I focused on the next file. I was
halfway through it when the partner who introduced me earlier
knocked on the door. I stood, as any courteous newbie
employee wanting his advance would do, but the partner
waved me away and pointed at Tempe, who excused herself
from the room like she was fine dining and needed to uphold
perfect etiquette. I figured they were discussing surveilling me
some more so I wouldn't break anything or knock somebody
out. Boxers scared people, and lawyers were no different. They
were sticklers for things like insurance and liability and all
those long complicated words that ended with "-ation."

I went on to the next file. And the next. And the next.

And then I hit pay dirt. Maybe because Tempe wasn't in
the room breathing over my shoulder. Or maybe because I was
just damn lucky sometimes.

I'd forgotten about the file Tempe tossed me before she left. Making it the thirtieth file to review for the day. Mr. James Dapper. A lot of people had the name James, but the Dapper surname seemed odd and out of sync somehow. The charging document said "Delivery of a Controlled Substance." Bingo. The guy's background included Possession of a Controlled Substance and Delivery of a Controlled Substance. Excellent. Six years spent in the Illinois Department of Corrections on the most recent drug conviction. Date of Sentence was two years ago. A pattern. Dapper was in his early thirties too, an age that would certainly attract somebody of Stevenson's caliber and wouldn't preclude romance. Checkmate. He was arrested playing a big poker game, and a shitload of drugs was recovered on his person. He posted a three-hundred-thousand-dollar D-bond.

But it wasn't until I found the names of the subjects on scene with Dapper that night that I knew that I was dealing with Vegas. Zelinski. Divac. Pekovic. A Serbian mob. Maybe not officially, but by association.

I looked for a phone number or an address. Nada. All the other files had contact numbers and addresses either on the front of the file or within the first few pages.

He didn't. Because he already had Stevenson's number, and she had his.

The sneaky bastard.

I tore through the file one more time, looking at the backs of all the pages. They stuck together easily, coffee the main culprit again. Midway through the file, I found it.

An address and a name.

That I already knew.

I stared at the yellow Post-it for a few seconds and wondered if Vegas was just crude or if this was my destiny. The stars aligning. The world slapping me to attention. My ass getting kicked to the canvas so I could get back up and get the job done.

I smiled.

Tempe came back. "Note to self: don't volunteer for super-human projects with the partners. It's the mother of all evils."

"I'm going on an investigation," I said. I stood up from my chair and grabbed the Vegas file.

"Fine, but you're on the clock. No naps and no detours. Don't make the news either."

I nodded and walked toward the door.

Before I made it out, Tempe said, "I have one ex. Doctor. He was my high school sweetheart. I found him in bed last year with one of his patients. That really did it for me."

18

The Windy City had a lot of seedy establishments in its two-hundred-plus-square-mile radius, but the Pink Purse took the cake. Founded over fifty years ago in the West Loop and frequented by a who's who of celebs, politicians, athletes, and other wannabes, the place prided itself on discreet pleasure twenty-four hours a day, seven days a week. It wasn't technically a brothel, but the subtext was clear. You pay to play.

James Dapper, aka Vegas, owned the place. I was sure of it. When I first found the Post-it in the file, it took me a minute to piece it together. The words "PP and Randolph" were scribbled in blue ink, followed by a couple of dollar signs. I knew of only one place on Randolph with those initials, and one place that was bringing in all that cash. The Pink Purse. I had once known the lay of the land in places like the Pink Purse quite well. I knew the rules and the score and the rhythm. I knew the good stories and the bad. Fame brought out a curious, almost stubborn thirst sometimes, and happy places were more than eager to quench it.

Now the Pink Purse was dead. No bouncers, no loud music destroying the ear canal, and no special lists to get in. Gentlemen and ladies alike could walk right in and grab a table front and center. Where the special people sat.

I walked in and found a spot off-stage. A couch with an unobstructed view of the performances. For back support.

Within seconds a perky Asian girl in a red thong and no top came up to me.

"How's it going there, handsome? I'm Sandy." She ran her hands down my chest all the way to my inner thighs. I was getting ticklish.

"Swell," I said. Sandy was good, but I didn't want to forget the task at hand.

She sat on my lap and grinded on me. I tried pushing her off, but she was ready. She caught both my hands, squeezed them in a vise grip, and grinded deeper, grinning like a Cheshire cat.

The proper etiquette at this point was to let it rain with some bills and place them in her thong. That would entice the female to pick up her game more and that in turn would entice the male to keep dropping bills. It was a business model rooted in sex that went back to the beginning of time and would surely go on till the end of time. A few more whispers and grins and bills would lead to special performances in back rooms. Muy bueno.

But I didn't have my advance and I doubted Sandy took credit.

"What's your name?" she said.

"Santa Claus."

Sandy shook her ass in a million different directions and whispered, "How's my Santa Claus doing?"

I was hard, and that was a recipe for disaster. It didn't bode well last time and wouldn't this time. I cut to the chase.

"Where's Vegas?" I asked.

"Who?" Sandy shook her ass faster as the music played louder. The songs were another ploy from the shysters in back. Dances went by the song, but they weren't standard length. The average song lasted between two and three minutes, while the Pink Purse version was only a hair over fifty-three seconds.

I grinded on Sandy as she grinded on me. This made her smile again, and I used the distraction to flip my hands on top of hers. I pulled her close and whispered in her ear, "Tell Vegas Santa Claus is here."

Sandy froze, then she slapped me in the face. "Fuck you, dude." She shuffled off, stage right into the back room.

I knew she wasn't getting Vegas. She was getting reinforcements. A stripper's reinforcements were the bouncers that stalked around the place like wannabe cops. The lack of them on the outside was a mirage of epic proportions. Armies huddled in back, analyzing cameras and back doors, and fucked the girls and got blowjobs for being protectors.

I figured at least seven of them would come out. That seemed appropriate for a midday shift at the Pink Purse. I saw about fifteen customers scattered around the place. Any one of them was a threat at any given time. Including me.

But this time I got the math wrong. Way wrong. *Twelve* bouncers came out. They pointed at me and motioned for me to get off the couch. I played dumb and stayed in my spot. I enjoyed the part that came next. When they surrounded me, I said, "What happened to Sandy?"

"Pay up, asshole, or get the fuck outta here," one of the bigger ones said. I tapped him as the leader of the bunch. Tall and bulky with a crew cut that said military dropout and bad exam- taker. The other guys just stood there and tensed their muscles like they were super cool.

"I get my advance today," I said.

The leader motioned for me to get up again.

I stayed put.

"Don't make this any harder than it needs to be. No money, no service. There's signs all over the place."

"I didn't get any service. I didn't even get hard."

The leader moved closer, a foot away from me now.

"Come any closer and you'll get knocked out all the way to the Idaho Potato Museum," I said. I stared the man down, but he didn't seem impressed. The stare-down made for great theater in the UFC or the WWE, but at the Pink Purse it looked stupid. We were like two overgrown jocks vying for the cheerleader who was vying for the theater nerd.

Then one of the other bouncers whispered something in the leader's ear, and everything changed.

"Do you box?" the leader said.

I slowly nodded, and then all the bouncers exhaled and took a couple steps back. The one who whispered snapped a pic of me.

"Sorry, man. We thought you were some asshole taking advantage of the girls. You know how it is in places like this. But a former champ is welcome here anytime. Bring your friends." The leader held out his hand, and for a moment I wanted to swat it away and give him a hard right to the face. A clean shot. But that would have been too easy.

I shook his hand.

"I'm here for Vegas," I said.

"Who?" The leader seemed genuinely confused.

"The owner. I have an appointment with him. I need to ask him a question."

The leader shook his head. "The owner died last week, and the GM is in Miami for the weekend."

"What's the GM's name?"

"Max Smith."

"Who's below the GM? I want to ask him a question."

"Me."

I knew that most bouncers were one fry short of a happy meal, but this one seemed well aware of the hierarchy of the Pink Purse. He wasn't bluffing. "Tell Max I stopped by," I said.

I got off the couch, and the rest of the bouncers parted like the Red Sea. As I walked toward the front door, some of them shadowboxed me. I grinned and kept moving. I preserved my knuckles and didn't have to break any noses. Thanks to the one hombre who'd recognized me. Things were looking up.

Just as I rounded the corner outside the Pink Purse, I heard a voice behind me say "Hey."

It was Sandy. Smoking a cigarette. With all her clothes on this time. "Super sorry about that in there," she said. "Can I get a picture for the Gram?" She took out her phone and craned her neck like a flamingo.

"Who?"

"Instagram, silly."

"I'm a D-lister now, but sure." Sandy tapped some things on her phone and in a quick, fluid motion that would make even Tempe jealous she held the phone up high and snapped some pics.

"Thanks so much. I can't believe you went to jail for something you didn't do. My brother did one month and he got out. He's a total pussy compared to you." She kissed me on the mouth. "Next time let me know you're coming and we'll get a private room. You were pretty hard back there."

I laughed. "I wasn't even warmed up yet." I hugged her and started walking away.

Then Sandy said, "Vegas owns the place on paper. Never runs it. Seen him once in the last two years. He came in, messed with the computer in back, did the books, and was gone. Ten minutes, tops. Didn't even try to flirt with us or anything. We've been through so many owners here and all of them wanna fuck at least once."

"What's he look like?" I asked.

"No clue. He came on Halloween dressed up as that Scream guy. Never took the mask off. None of the girls said anything. We like our tips."

"Where is he now?"

"He's a ghost. Heard he lived with this lawyer in River North for a while, then things went south. He bought a gun shop and became one of those bumper-sticker second-amendment losers. Wouldn't surprise me one bit. As long as the checks keep coming, who's complaining?"

Sandy told me she had to get back to work. A soccer team from Boston was coming in. She tossed her cigarette butt and was gone.

And before I could head out myself, I felt cold steel on the back of my head, and everything went black.

19

I woke up in a dumpster—and a pile of piss and pizza. My hair had Ramen noodles in it and someone had written "You suck" in Sharpie on my elbow. My phone was still on me and my Chelsea boots too, so overall I dubbed the beatdown a success. Whoever connected the steel object with my skull had wanted to send a message—one that fell short of fatal. I knew the difference. I'd seen it on the inside. All it took was one swipe to the carotid artery with a makeshift razor and adios amigo. This beatdown was civil.

I got up and pulled the noodles out of my hair. There were five long curly strands that put Rapunzel to shame. Then I stretched my neck out and took in my surroundings. I hadn't been out for long because it was still daylight outside, but I wasn't by the Pink Purse anymore. My ass had been dumped in an alley that faced the back of a Thai restaurant and a car insurance place. I looked up, then left, then right. And I found it.

A security camera. Looking right down at the dumpster that I now called home.

Then I spotted another looking virtually at the same spot. If I was lucky, both cameras worked and had captured the moment of truth.

I walked around to the front of the businesses and started with the car insurance place. A homeless man inside asked if there was special insurance for DUI drivers. When they broke down all the procedures and deductibles the homeless man spit out some alien speak and stormed out.

"May I help you sir?" the bubbly front desk girl asked.

"Is the security camera outside your business in the upper right-hand corner of the roof working?"

The bubbly girl looked at me like I had herpes. "Are you a cop?"

"I'm a concerned citizen who has a personal interest in fighting systematic abuse in the area."

"I can't give out personal business information without a badge."

I pulled out my razor-thin wallet and handed her my expired driver's license. She looked it up and down, frowned, then looked at me like a lightbulb went off.

"Did you go to Lane Tech with Mickey Caruso? He's my brother. Played football."

I flashed my pearly whites. "I was the waterboy. Your bro was real good." Ha ha.

The bubbly girl smiled, then frowned. "The cameras have been down for weeks. I keep telling my boss to fix them, but he's too preoccupied with his new mistress. We had a pizza rat wreaking havoc back there last week."

"What color was he?"

"I don't know. Rats are disgusting."

"I'll put in a good word if I come across him."

"Can I get a picture? My brother won't believe it."

"No can do. My knee is singing songs right now. Must rest."

I tried the Thai restaurant next. The minute I walked in my stomach complained about my negligence. I was used to eating infrequent meals at infrequent times over the last twelve years, but I knew that I now needed to give my stomach some much needed TLC. My body was my temple, and to perform at optimum level I needed to treat it as such. Sal was always on my case telling me cheeseburgers didn't make champions but greens did. We had philosophical differences at the time, but I wasn't getting any younger, and Sal was on the money.

"How many?" the hostess asked.

"One. I'll take the fourth booth from the right and a meeting with your manager."

She shook her head. "The manager is out, sir. Don't know when he'll be back."

"Who's the second guy in charge?"

"Why?"

"Is the security camera outside your business in the upper left-hand corner of your roof working?"

She frowned. "Just a minute, sir." She put down a menu and shuffled back to the kitchen. I knew the manager was back there, but I played it cool. The average human avoids confrontation and deflects and lies to save face. I was the exact opposite. I relished confrontation and enjoyed the uncertainty that came with it. If the hostess summoned some Jackie Chan fighters I'd be ready to mingle and take names.

I examined the art on the walls. The restaurant had an eclectic display of murals and paintings. Muy bueno. They gave it a homey feel that added to the ambiance.

I took out my phone and checked for missed calls. Nada. Tempe wasn't on my case yet, but it was only a matter of time before she called and complained that I was taking advantage on the clock. I'd tell her I was still investigating furiously.

The hostess came back and picked up a menu. "Sir, your table. The manager is on his way."

She led me to an oval-shaped booth with purple dragons on it. I thanked her and analyzed the menu. I hadn't thought this far ahead because I'd expected to either be denied straight out or to get confirmation on the camera capture. I had two dollars and fifty-eight cents left in my wallet. As I looked at the menu, I realized I was done, unless I asked for something on the kids' menu. The chocolatey explosions sounded excellent. I attacked the bread rolls and downed some water. When the waitress came I told her I needed more time.

Then a skinny Asian man with glasses sat down across from me.

"Are you going to order something or cause a ruckus in my beautiful restaurant?"

I pointed to the beverages list. "There's nothing under two-sixty here."

"I can't keep the lights on like that." The manager laughed. "Which police department are you with?"

"The department of unfinished business. Your cameras captured a beatdown and I want to get to the bottom of it."

"Where's your badge?"

"I left it at home."

The manager shook his head. "Unless you have a badge or a subpoena I can't give you anything. Otherwise every customer with every little problem would come in here asking for the moon. I can't accommodate that. No way."

"I'll give you an autograph."

"For what?"

"You can put it on Twitter and over there where the murals are. People will come in and ooh and ahh about it and ask how you got the autograph. You'll tell them I'm a very nice customer who comes in a lot. I love Thai."

"Who the hell are you?"

"Lance Gedrin."

"Means nothing to me."

"The boxer."

"Still nothing."

"The champ who went down for murder. A bogus one."

"Have no idea."

I looked around the place for a TV. It was five o'clock, and the evening news would have something. I looked past the counter and past the bathrooms and past the waiting area and spotted a small TV right in front of the kitchen. Some of the people at the counter could see it and so could some of the kitchen staff.

The first story was about Stine. The cops were still investigating. Good.

The second was about Stevenson. No leads.

Then my mug shot flashed on the screen.

"There," I said, pointing to the TV.

The manager got up from the booth and walked to the TV. I couldn't see the subtitles from where I was, but he surely could. When the news anchors transitioned to a clip of cats dancing, he returned.

"Very good. I know now. You're the stupid boxer who got hit in the head so many times, went to jail, got out, and is trying to be a cop now. Every day, nothing but drama here. I should have opened a pizza shop."

"Deep dish is the best. Get a few ovens, a delivery boy, a couple cooks and you're good. Low overhead, señor."

The manager laughed like a hyena, then said, "Why do you want the tape? What new crimes are you going to commit with it?"

I told him about finding Stevenson and what she meant to my case. I didn't hold back.

The manager looked wistfully outside the front window. "This place belonged to my grandfather, my father, and now me. You lose your family, you gotta fight for them. To the death. Come on back."

20

I took another bread roll and followed the manager into a dusty room. Cardboard boxes lined all four walls, and a brown folding table sat in the middle, holding a monitor that looked more ancient than the art out front. Beside it was a beige VHS player. For the first time in the last week I felt perfectly at home.

The manager pointed. The tapes are on the left side."

"These are fine machines," I said.

"The best. My son is bugging me to go to some cloud, but I refuse. Too complicated."

The manager returned to the front, and I took the first VHS tape, labeled "Security," and popped it in the player. It made some weird noises for a few seconds, then the monitor came to life and the screen split into halves. One half showed the front of the restaurant and the other half the alley in back. I couldn't figure out the date and time because there were no timestamps, so I pressed a button on the player and fast-forwarded for a minute, making hundreds of people go in and out of the place faster than Usain Bolt. Business was booming. I slowed it down again when I saw activity out back. Just a couple cooks smoking and some waitresses arguing with their phones. I fast-forwarded again and saw more of the same.

I tried another tape, this one labeled "Security Next." Maybe the cloud would help for naming and clarity's sake. If there were ever any investigations involving the restaurant, these tapes would be a cop's worst nightmare.

This tape had more drama. An argument out back led to a fistfight. Somebody got slapped, and the manager broke it up and shooed them back to the kitchen. No medical attention. Par for the course in a high-volume place.

Soon I was putting in a tape labeled "Security 3." More of the same faces, the same actions. And then I found what I was looking for.

The pizza rat. Taking away a large slice of sausage pizza. Carb heaven.

Then I saw Sandy.

And me.

I must have been really concussed because apparently I was still right around the corner from the Pink Purse and hadn't realized it till now. Sandy was smoking a cigarette and oozing sex the way Marilyn Monroe did. And the camera didn't do her justice. I'd take those lips in person any day of the week.

She and I talked for a bit, then Sandy stubbed her cigarette out with her shoe and left.

And I got my ass kicked.

A man in a beanie came up behind me and hit me with a pipe. I went down like a bag of rocks. Sal would have torn a neck muscle screaming if he'd seen the highlight. The man wasn't that big, but he was agile—a runner maybe, or extreme sports enthusiast. He wore black joggers, a long-sleeved gray Henley, and black Nikes. He would have stood out on a normal May day in the Windy City, but today was one of those days where winter didn't want to call it quits. It was in the low forties, but felt a lot colder. I didn't miss Chicago weather one bit. Summer to fall to winter to spring to winter again in a heartbeat. No bueno.

The beanie man dragged me to the dumpster and tossed me in. Then he picked up some noodles and tossed them over my face the way Emeril yells "BAM!" with his signature dishes. The beanie man looked both ways and bounced outta there.

I played the video ten times start to finish, but I never got a clear view of the man's face. The guy was a pro, and he knew which camera was working. Even in slow-mo, I got nothing.

Or so I thought.

In one frame of the video I picked up a sliver of a forearm covered in tattoos. A lot of them. I tried to zoom in, but it only distorted the picture. I pulled back and re-watched, focusing on just the forearm this time.

I recognized one of the tattoos. It was the same one Stevenson had. The shark from hell. I took out my phone and snapped some pics.

The manager came back. "Any luck, champ?"

"Can I zoom in some more on this video?"

He shook his head. "Maybe in the cloud, but not here. Everything's screwed up."

"How do I take a video of this video? On my phone?"

The manager took my phone and played around with it. He too was confused by tech. We were two dinosaurs in a non-dinosaur world. But he figured it out and took a video of the video.

"There. Decent quality."

"I've got all I need," I said.

I thanked him and we shook hands. He promised to host a party for me if I ever had a fight again. I told him that was the plan, but not in the cards right now. I needed an extended camp to shake off the rust and avoid colossal embar-rassment.

As I walked out of the restaurant, I realized that I needed to make one more stop before I checked back in at work. I should have done it sooner, but I'd been biding my time. Waiting for the perfect moment. But now...it had to be done.

21

S tine's place was seven blocks east and two blocks north. Her license was still valid, and the address on it stood in the heart of Bucktown. I'd expected Gold Coast or River North, but apparently reporters didn't make the green that lawyers did. The plan was to get inside and draw as little attention as possible. CPD was investigating, which meant there was a possibility they were still turning Stine's home upside down, analyzing it for any clues that might make some sense of what had happened. I wasn't about to tell CPD what I knew, so I'd stay in the shadows. If anybody got too cute I'd plead ignorance and then the fifth. That was a sound plan.

I knew the cops wouldn't let up. High-profile cases ebbed and flowed like all the others, but the pressure meter was nothing like all the others. Jobs were on the line when the public fell in love with the victim. Stine wasn't a huge celebrity, but she *was* a known commodity. And a known commodity meant more eyeballs watching everything. Including me.

If I was lucky, the officers were done processing her home and notifying her next of kin. The investigation would shift to the places that Stine frequented and the people that she most spent time with. Ex-lovers, ex-coworkers, current lovers, current coworkers. The never-ending cycle of human flesh. The revolving door of personalities and quirks. Reporters had so many contacts and the cops had so many leads to chase down.

As I walked past an ice cream shop I felt a sudden pang of guilt that I was with Stine for her last breath and her family wasn't. One moment your girl is lighting up the screen getting closer and closer to the big time in New York, and the next a fat cop named Carl with donut stains on his shirt shows up at your door and says your daughter is in a box.

Damn.

I walked past a rollerblading rink, an abandoned factory, and a prepaid cell phone store. Bucktown was an interesting mix of culture. I walked another block and found Stine's place. Nestled between two old school buildings and diagonal to a Golden Nugget pancake house, her place screamed new construction. Stine was smart. She wanted luxury city living at affordable suburban prices. From the looks of it, she got in early and schooled the system with a solid living space.

I walked across the street and past the older building on the left. As I stopped to look around, a Corgi came up and sniffed me. The Corgi's owner smiled, and I returned it. I didn't see any suits or badges. No marked cars. No unmarked Crown Vics.

I took Stine's keys from my pocket and went to the small black gate at the front of the property. The key didn't work on the first try, but try again and you shall succeed. The lock opened on the second try, and I took five steps up to the front door and used the same key to get in. Mailboxes on both sides ran down a long hallway, leading to a beige elevator in the middle. The key that worked so well with the gate and front door didn't fare as well with the mailbox. If I found the right key later, I'd come back.

I took the elevator to the third floor, where all was quiet. I found unit 303 and listened for movement on the other side. When I heard nothing, I put the key in the door and hoped that nothing would jump me from the other side. The key worked, making me three for four, and I walked in without suffering any bodily harm.

But I had celebrated too quickly.

Cats.

I smelled them immediately, and I wanted to curl up and vomit. Not only was I super allergic to cats, I genuinely didn't like them. Their eyes freaked the hell out of me and their independent cabinet-surfing ways were very annoying. But a job was a job. I locked the door behind me and ignored the three cats that came up and rubbed against my leg, whining and crying.

Stine's place was awesome. Modern design with two bedrooms, nice windows, stellar kitchen decor and furniture. Even the rugs were brand new. As I stood there for a moment taking it all in, the three cats gave up on me and sprang away onto the furniture like kangaroos. I was convinced they were Air Jordan incarnate.

I went to work.

I rifled through all the kitchen cabinets and drawers. Nada. I looked in, out, around, left, right, and under all the furniture. I checked the windows, the window sills, the balcony, the little cookie jars on the counter, the refrigerator magnets, the little drawer under the oven, the fridge, the freezer, and even under the soil of all the potted plants in the living room.

I came up empty.

I moved on to the guest bedroom. There were four more cats, and they were having a cage match. They cried and clawed at each other, exposing their teeth. I tiptoed around them and checked under the bed, the covers, in between the mattress and the box spring. Nope. I checked the closet, and found nothing but a foam roller and a yoga mat. The secrets to longevity.

I checked the hallway closet, the guest coat closet, and the guest bathroom.

Then I went to the master bedroom, and stopped short. I took out my phone and started taking pictures. I had a lot of work to do.

22

Stine was a hoarder, plain and simple. Her bed was stacked high with notebooks, legal pads, folders, Post-it Notes, pens, pencils, stencils, and photos.

Hundreds of them.

I shut the door behind me to prevent a cat attack, and I analyzed the contents of the bed. There were crossword puzzles and scribbled music lyrics and photos of Stine with her family. It looked like she was making a collage for art class. I pushed the top layer to the side, and the next layer was all work-related.

One case got top billing, and it wasn't Stevenson's—it was mine. There were pictures of Amy Pako in high school, in college, and right before her residency. Her smile was absolutely beautiful, conveying innocence and youth and a future filled with potential. Until she was raped and murdered and tossed like a rag doll to the pigs on I-57. A boy and his beagle found her left arm first, then her kneecaps.

I knew the pictures better than my DOB and social security number. They were paraded before my trial, during my trial, and long after my trial. Together they were the *sine qua non* of the disintegration of due process. I remember sitting in court doing my best to ignore them, as if they would somehow disappear like Houdini. Stevenson said to look at them would suggest I was acknowledging my sadistic kill, but to not look at them would suggest I was a complete psychopath. Find the middle ground. So I'd steal a glance at them for a second and go back to my notes at the defense table. Some good that did.

Next to the Pako pictures were shots of me being taken out of Sal's gym in cuffs, in court whispering things to Stevenson, and on the rec yard. I was impressed with the rec yard shots because they were from a bunch of angles, which must have taken some real work. Extreme coordination and concentration. Hail the photographer. I looked for pictures of me benching heavy weight with Murdock, but to my dismay there were none. I found a court sketch of me drinking a plastic cup of water; the artist had a keen eye for detail and hues. I was tempted to pocket it, but CPD's finest could do a second pass of the place, and if they'd already logged the photo and came back to find it missing, a massive coronary was on the horizon. I looked at a few more photos, these showing Stevenson doing a press conference. Her press conferences were legendary and viral before there ever was such a thing.

Next to the pictures were news articles on the case, and on Stevenson's efforts to free me. Stine had drawn some boogers on one of Stevenson's pictures, so that summed up the relationship. I read some of the articles before realizing I'd already read them on the inside. The mind doth forget sometimes.

I looked under Stine's bed, fully expecting another cat to fly out and scratch me to death. No cat, but nothing else either.

But in her closet, I found a big whiteboard on wheels. A large Venn diagram filled the entire board. Jackpot. One circle was labeled "Stevenson," a second circle "Zemun," and the overlapping area in the middle was labeled "Connects." A photo was in the Stevenson circle—a picture of me during my first title run. An aesthetic shot by a great ringside photographer. Stevenson's photo was in the circle too, followed by two sheets from a yellow pad, listing a handwritten timeline. I took out my phone and snapped as many pics as I could, in case the board went Houdini later.

May 24

First District vacates Gedrin's conviction. Case reversed and remanded back to the trial court for further proceedings. Reached Gertrude for comment. She texted back that emergency motion for bond review to follow. Good chance Gedrin gets out pending possible retrial. Ball in State's court. Have 10 days from date of order to decide whether to retry the case.

May 25.

Emergency motion to review bond heard. State is fighting this tooth and nail. Brought five different lawyers to argue against bail. Ten detectives stacked the jury box in support of vic Amy Pako. Pako's family not in court. Hearing went on for over an hour. Judge ultimately granted it, with an exasperated look on his face. Texted Gertrude congrats afterward. She replied with one of those form "thanks" texts. Nothing further.

May 26

Gertrude doesn't show up to work and midday associate Kayla Tempe calls it in. CPD is all over this. I got the call and every network too. I spoke to a secretary before the firm shut down all talks with the media. Secretary said that Gertrude went silent right after the victory yesterday. No calls, texts... firm thought she was out celebrating the win. But then she didn't show up to work next day and all hell broke loose. Missing persons investigation or murder? Seems super fishy. At 6:30PM I called the firm again to get an official comment from Kayla Tempe. Immediately shut down by somebody in firm's PR department. Bullshit statement issued about cooperating with authorities and letting them handle the investigation. I don't trust Kayla Tempe. She blew up at our office one time over DUI client. Weird, annoying one.

MAY 27

Secretary gets fired from the firm (probably because she went off the record with me and other outlets). She then agrees to go on the record with us. Firm finds out and threatens this paper with litigation. Paper tells me to drop it because there's no independent corroboration, and I have no choice but to listen. I like getting paid. I get Kayla Tempe's number from barrister Pete. I text Kayla trying to get a statement. She sends a bitchy reply back. "See our rules and regs on media matters lady. Don't mess with us. We have clients to serve."

THAT EVENING, interns find possible Gertrude-Vegas connection. Vegas owns a gun shop in Kentucky. Gertrude defended him on drug charges a while back. Rumored mobster ties for the man. She loses the case. Vegas does about one year on a six-year bid. Gun shop suddenly closes per wits in Kentucky on May 24, day before Gertrude goes missing. Motive to kill her.

. . .

MAY 28

Investigation ongoing. CPD media liaison floating to outlets that they're looking at some sex offenders from the area. Easy out. Keep looking.

MAY 29

Investigation ongoing. Sent a PI to try and track Vegas. Nothing yet. Maybe he's hiding somewhere.

MAY 30

Court reporter confirms that Vegas and Gertrude were fucking. When case was going on, she spotted them making out in the hallway and Vegas pushed her up against a wall. If she didn't walk by, they would have fully done the deed right then and there. Lawyers can't contain that insane sex drive I guess. Vegas is prime suspect right now. Nothing else real plausible.

MAY 31

Gedrin shows up at firm looking for Gertrude. Gertrude's most recent client. Keep him around. He would also make for a great exclusive. Human interest angle piece. What Gertrude was like outside the well of the courtroom.

JUNE 1

PI found some Vegas business ties. Will accompany him on location to check it out.

. . .

THE TIMELINE WAS VERY easy to follow, and it showed Stine's dedication. She chased the story till the very moment she died. She was onto Vegas's business ties like I was. I owed it to her to get to the bottom of all of it. Maybe the canned secretary had more answers. Maybe I'd ask Tempe some roundabout questions about her.

The Zemun circle wasn't as complete. All it said was "Serbian Gang." I already knew there was some sort of Serbian connection to the case, and gang vs. mob semantics didn't really matter. But I made a note to learn more about the Zemun. Maybe their customs and rituals hinted at something bigger. I knew Stevenson hung around Serbian types and Stine reported on Serbian types, but that wouldn't get the job done. I was sparring here instead of fighting for the title.

The overlap between the two circles said, "Did Vegas indoctrinate her in the gang?"

And that was it. Everything Stine knew.

I searched the rest of the place anyway, and came up empty. I wheeled the whiteboard back into the closet and tried to rearrange everything just the way Stine had it. A hoarder wouldn't notice a difference, but Chicago's finest probably would.

Just when I finished putting everything away, the front door opened.

23

I managed to hide under the bed. Whoever came in dropped keys on the hardwood floor before picking them up again. Loud footsteps went to the kitchen, then the guest bedroom. Then the bathroom for a few minutes. Then down the hall.

To the master bedroom where I was hiding.

I tend to get leg cramps in small spaces. Doesn't matter if I'm fully stretched or crouched somewhere. And when my hammies tighten up like an anaconda, I can't help myself—my syllables come out faster than a cheetah on the prowl. Sometimes I make perfect sense. Other times people need a copy of Merriam-Webster to make sense of it all. The hammies are truly unusual creatures.

Right when the footsteps came into the bedroom, my right leg became a sliver of sedimentary rock. Fuck. No dictionary needed. I reached back with my right hand and squeezed my right hamstring like it was a piece of bubble wrap. Sometimes this made the pain go away and I'd live to fight another day. Most of the time it did jack shit. Like now. My hammy only tightened more, and I rolled my ankle around hoping that would help.

The footsteps went to the desk next to the bed. I peeked under the bed skirt and saw New Balance trainers, blue with a hint of green. An excellent color combo. The shoes moved around the desk, a drawer slid open, and papers shuffled. Then the shoes moved to the master bathroom for no more than thirty seconds, before returning to the hallway.

I was in the clear.

I exhaled deeply and smiled.

Then a voice said, "Get the fuck out right now or you're going to jail."

I couldn't take it anymore. My cramps got the best of me and I rolled out from the under the bed screaming "Rocky Marciano!" I clutched my right leg and pushed it outward like I was doing the wave. Nada. My leg was an out-of-order turn signal. I closed my eyes and counted to twelve. Visualization made all the difference sometimes.

Five. Seven. Nine. Eleven.

Twelve.

The pain was gone.

When I opened my eyes, a super hot woman was pointing a gun right at my face. She was close to six feet tall with fuchsia hair, and she looked like she ate breakfast, lunch, and dinner at the gym.

"Speak or I pull the trigger," she said.

"I don't see a license for that fine piece of steel," I said.

"I can take my cop badge and shove it up your ass if you like."

"What's your star number and unit of assignment?" I asked. The woman was in running gear. Unless CPD lowered their standards since I got out, no way was this chick with Team Blue.

"I'm Colorado PD. We do things differently out west. Who the fuck are you?" She stepped closer, keeping the gun trained on me.

I said, "Lance Gedrin. Pancake enthusiast and champion boxer dude."

She moved even closer. I've had the distinct pleasure of standing in front of the barrel of a gun three times in my life. Each time the gun holder was drunk and didn't realize he had no bullets. This time marked the fourth. I couldn't pick odds with this one. We were in Bucktown.

"Is that bullshit supposed to put my guard down?" she said. "Ain't working, man."

"The truth hurts. I love pancakes and bashing people's brains in. Legally. Bright lights. The squared circle. Let's try this again. I'm Lance Gedrin. Former heavyweight champion boxer who went down twelve years for a murder I didn't commit. Maybe you've seen the news, or do you Colorado cops just ski all day and shit?"

The woman gave me a death stare, and for a moment I thought I was looking at Stine's doppelgänger. Then she put the gun down. "That doesn't explain why you're in my sister's place. I'm Kate Decker. Erin's older sister. Married twice, but kept my asshole first husband's name."

"They say second time's the charm."

"It's third time actually. I can see why my sister liked you."

"She was special," I said.

"Were you fucking her?"

"No. Our relationship was business-oriented. She wanted my story." I sat on the edge of the bed.

Decker put the gun in the back of her pants. "I'm here to pick up her things," she said. "Find some nice pictures and trinkets for the funeral. The cops haven't released the body yet.

But when they do it's gonna be a shit-show. Half the city will show up."

"She was a great reporter," I said. "Tenacious but fair."

"Yeah. Don't mean much now." Decker went over to the desk again and put some things in her pocket.

"Pull some strings," I said. "Get the asshole who did this."

"I have no pull with this department. CPD is too damned good apparently. I tried speaking to the detectives about the evidence and they treated me like some banger carjacking people. Fucking assholes."

"If you want it done right, you have to do it yourself," I said. "I'm gonna find out who did this to her, and there's gonna be hell to pay."

"Is that a threat?"

"It's a promise."

"Yeah? I appreciate the concern, but what the hell are you gonna do without the resources? You have a gun?"

"No."

"You have a Taser?"

"No."

"How 'bout a car with police radio?"

"Hell no."

"You know how to detain somebody?"

"A little bit."

"What kind of training do you have in case your life is on the line?"

"I've been boxing since I was ten years old. I can handle it."

Decker shook her head. "Boxing means shit when some-one's trying to stab you in the neck and someone else is going for your blind spot."

"I'll be ready. I'll have one of those vicious dogs to take him down. Someone like Henri."

"Who?"

"Henri. The Doberman. Everybody will cower in fear when they see him."

"Whatever. You must have a lot of concussions, boxer dude." Decker finished up with the photos and went to the living room. I followed. All the cats came out and rubbed against Decker's shoes.

"I hate cats," I said.

"Me too. But my sister was crazy about them."

"They need a forever home. Or a furrever home. Get it?"

"Yeah. I'll call animal control and be done with it. Please leave. You seem like a decent guy, but my family needs some space now."

"Cool. I'll be gone like the wind in the willows. But one question."

"What?"

"Have you heard of the Zemun?"

"Why?"

"You have all the resources. And a badge."

"What does this have to do with my sister?"

"Everything."

Decker looked me up and down like I had the plague. The bags under her eyes poked at me like little insect tendrils.

"Tell me," she said.

I told her all about Stevenson, and Stine's efforts to find her. I included all the important parts and left out all the boring parts and the ones that would lead a reasonable person to believe I was somehow involved. Decker didn't show any emotion as I spoke. Cops were by nature emotionless beings. By the book and rote. It came with the territory and helped them catch really bad hombres who made your blood run cold at night. Waterworks never got any commendations.

When I was all done, Decker sighed and said, "The Zemun are small in scale, but ruthless like all the rest. They came from

Belgrade and are very communal and cannibalistic in nature. We got a couple cases like that in Denver. Dead bodies burned in a car after some local beef. At the lab, the coroner said the bodies were eaten first before being placed in the car. Sick fucks. Both cases were traced back to some billionaire honcho in Tokyo who calls all the shots, but nobody can pin him with anything."

"What's his name?"

"Don't know. Nobody can get a name on this guy or connect him to anything solid. Like the Teflon Don. Nothing sticks. He's a smooth operator. Tats, literature, followers. That's the name of the game. Always."

"What kind of literature?"

"Every gang follows a bible. A manual with some bullshit ideologies and customs. Makes no sense to us, but to them it's perfection that'll lead them to the promised land. Wars have been started on the streets because of that shit. Children have been killed for no reason. Innocent passersby. The destruction never ends."

I said, "Where can I get a copy?"

Decker shrugged. "Hell if I know. We gave that shit to the prosecutor on one of the cases and it's buried in some vault now. Even if you dig it up it wouldn't be much help. Unless you're one of them. These assholes are constantly evolving. Do me a favor. Don't go chasing ghosts you can't catch."

"I'll catch them."

"Says the boxer with the leg cramps. Rocky Marciano? Tyson was the best and there's no way around it."

"But Marciano was undefeated," I said. "Only heavyweight ever. Brute power and skill."

Decker smiled. "You're funny. But funny will get you killed on these streets in a heartbeat. Let the cops handle this. It may

GREG GOUNTANIS

take some time, but they'll get them eventually. I can only hope they're as dedicated here as we are out in the mountains."

I sneezed. The cats were getting to me. "I've been through things I wouldn't wish on my worst enemy. I'm not backing down till I get answers."

Decker just held out her hand. "Keys."

"Oh, yeah." I took out Stine's keys and dropped them in Decker's palm.

"When did she give you these?"

"At the Cubs game."

"Cool."

Even though Decker and Stine were family, I didn't trust her enough to give her all the facts. And I kept Stine's wallet. We exchanged numbers. As I walked out the door I turned and said, "Don't give up on her."

Decker picked up one of the cats and stroked her. She purred and wanted more. "You never give up on your blood, but after a while the logical cop side of you takes over and you realize that the more time that goes by, the more time the killer is getting across the border or getting on a plane and gone for good. All it takes is cash and a little head start. I wasn't super close with my sister, but I'd come up here twice a year and we'd talk about work and family and guys and all that shit. It was nice. I'm gonna find the asshole who did this and let him know how we Colorado cops operate. If you find him first, knock him out so he never wakes up."

I smiled. "Easy peasy."

24

I logged nine hours and twenty-four minutes of investigation on my first day at the firm. I was a bona fide Sherlock Holmes minus the pipe. I didn't know if the partners would ask for a mileage log or a map of my travels, but I had it all in my frontal cortex. The mind was a beautiful thing.

As I walked into the firm, the reporters were either in hiding or eating dinner. The trucks were gone. The sun, too. I took the elevator up to the fifteenth floor and was greeted by a bunch of suits clutching briefcases and umbrellas for fashion. I didn't recognize any of them, and they didn't recognize me. They hadn't been in the morning meeting either, so my money was on them being overworked and harried associates commingling to drown their sorrows. Ale therapy at its finest. I nodded to ghosts and admired the artwork again.

The secretary was gone, but this time I knew the layout of the place. I went straight to Tempe's office and knocked on the door. I was met with silence, so I tried the handle. It was locked, but I wouldn't give up that easy. I peered through the windows. I pressed my face up against the glass and made noises with rhythm and excellent musicality. No dice. She wasn't there.

"We all thought you quit."

I turned to find Tempe right behind me. She wasn't wearing a suit anymore. She wore even tighter jeans than last night, along with a bright-red University of Wisconsin Badgers hoodie. I was curious if her body was well insulated underneath. If the time was right, I'd do a thorough inspection.

"An investigation is best done by leaving no stone unturned."

Tempe unlocked her door and led me into her office. Now that the sun was gone, the city lights bounced off the walls and illuminated the space beautifully. I could get used to the view. Despite the package of billable hours that came with it, there was something to be said about nightlife with an urban populace. Beware temptation.

Tempe sat behind her desk, and I took one of the client chairs.

"Well, shoot," she said. "What stones did you unturn?"

"Vegas owns the Pink Purse, but on the down-low. He's on paper, but never shows."

"The first place you go on an investigation is to see some tits and ass? The partners are going to kill me."

"There's something to be said about the ambiance and choreography of the dances. The effort is sublime and there's a lot of emotion and meaning behind it if you pay attention. Vegas thinks he can hide, but I've got him. No doubt."

Tempe rolled her eyes. "Did you get this epiphany before or after you got a special dance?"

I smiled. "Before *and* after. You must like special dances."

Tempe grinned. "Depends on who's giving them."

"I'll bet." I'd give her special dances till my shoes wore out and my hammies said no. I wanted to ask her out on a proper second date first, but rules are meant to be broken sometimes.

"It's another dead end," Tempe said. "So what, Gertrude repped wealthy people. We're a high-profile firm. Duh."

"Why would a former client up and disappear like that? A businessman no less. They seek the limelight the way a junkie seeks the needle. They wanna build their business off the sweaty backs of others and take all the credit when it pops. Vegas wanted in Stevenson's pants on top of it. Seems like she was game. He had the motive. He owned a gun shop in Kentucky too."

Tempe closed her eyes. "Your investigation led you to Kentucky?"

I realized I'd spilled some of Stine's recon. I didn't like putting all my cards on the table at once, but I had to in good faith justify my existence to my employer. To eat. To sleep. And to get to the Space Needle when the time was right. Tempe knew about Vegas, but now she knew about Kentucky. Maybe it was for the best.

"A good investigator pursues leads both foreign and domestic," I said.

"And a good journalist never reveals her sources." Lawyers were always one step ahead. Damn.

"She was a great one. That's for sure."

"Until somebody put a bullet in her head on the side of the road and nobody gave a shit." Tempe frowned.

"Absolutely terrible."

Tempe said nothing. Then she reached under her desk and pulled out a big envelope.

"While you were out analyzing thongs, I was pulling strings with the higher-ups. Here's your advance. Two weeks' pay. The firm couldn't justify paying you more up front when you haven't done shit. They see you as a huge liability. No experience other than breaking skulls. They made it clear to me that this is a trial basis kind of thing. Better keep pounding the pavement and doing what you're told. No questions asked."

"I love experiments, and I always bring my A game. Don't hate." I took the envelope from Tempe and cradled it like my heavyweight title the first time. It was a baby bird in my arms, and I wasn't letting go. I analyzed the check in front of Tempe just to make sure the partners weren't playing games. All there. I was moving on up. I couldn't stay at the Four Seasons, but I could certainly stay away from the clearance rack.

"What happened to your face?" Tempe asked.

"Somebody engaged me in a long conversation. He didn't see it my way." I touched my face and realized I still had a bruise on my right cheekbone. Must be from when I crumpled to the concrete in a pile of awesome noodles. Decker hadn't mentioned it, but leave it to Tempe.

"Let me get you some ice for that."

She got up from her desk and retrieved an ice pack from a mini-fridge. She tossed it to me, and when I put it on my face, I felt immediate relief. A lifetime in the ring makes you numb to bumps and bruises, but ice says hello every time.

I was hungry and tired, but Tempe was just getting started.

"I need that tie back," she said. "Now that you've met the masses, you can dress down a little bit."

"Swell. Come and get it." I gave Tempe a sly smile, and she returned it again. Lucky was my middle name these days. I didn't want it to stop.

And it didn't.

Tempe came up to me and ran her hands all the way down my chest again. This time she didn't fix my tie, but instead undid it and placed it around the nape of my neck. She pulled me super close and whispered, "You're so much trouble. You know that?"

"I retired that surname a long time ago."

Tempe laughed and put her hands on my face. They were soft and gentle and they sent jolts of electricity all through my body. I closed my eyes, and her lips touched mine. They stayed that way for a while, then were replaced by her finger.

"Wait," she said.

Her hands left my body and she went to the door. She locked it, then pressed a button for the shutters. The room went dark, but I could see everything I needed.

Tempe took the tie from me and put it back in her closet. She spent a lot of time reorganizing so I decided to help her out. She appreciated it. I put my hands on her hips and pulled her close. I kissed her neck. Tempe made the next move. And I made the one after that. We alternated and didn't keep score. We didn't care. We fucked for an eternity right there in her office. We spoke in code, but this time we both understood each other. We asked all the right questions and had all the right answers. When it was all said and done, Tempe had the edge in the cardio department. I was still tired from my investigation.

Afterward, we sat there for two minutes in the post-coital glow.

I said nothing.

Tempe said nothing.

Then somebody knocked on the door, and we heard footsteps down the hall. Followed by more footsteps. Then screams. Then somebody said, "Oh my god."

I dressed first. Tempe took her time.

When she opened the door, an employee said, "Come quick."

"It's always *something* after hours," Tempe said. "Geez."

We walked out of the office together. She held my hand for

a second but released it the moment she saw another face at the firm. I didn't mind. We were two travelers at O'Hare that would eventually find the right terminal for our expedition. We went to the break room and had to push past a crowd to get to the TV. I didn't even look at the headline on the screen, because I knew already.

I was being retried for Amy Pako's murder.

25

Cook County State's Attorney Evangelos Carpetopoulos did the honors. He stood behind a podium flanked by an army of supporters. He wore a navy-blue suit, white shirt, and red paisley tie, and his hair was well-coiffed, but the great ensemble couldn't hide his portly cheeks and stubborn belly.

I sat all the way in the back of the break room by the garbage cans. I should've brought popcorn for the spectacle. Instead I sipped on a water bottle and tried not to yawn through the shit-show that I was about to see. Tempe was in front whispering things to her coworkers and not making eye contact with me.

Carpetopoulos must not have been used to the media glare, because before he even began his opening remarks he dropped a few papers and spilled a glass of water behind the podium. And when he went to pick up the glass it slipped out of his hand and shattered. He apologized profusely as he fixed his tie, and the sharks ate up every second of it. The Nielsen overnights were going to be huge.

"Thank you all for coming out late this evening. I know rush hour was particularly bad. Today, on behalf of the Cook County State's Attorney's Office, I would like to formally announce that we will be retrying Lance Gedrin for the murder of Amy Pako. As you all know, his conviction was vacated on appeal last week, and the court gave us a one-week deadline to decide whether to retry Mr. Gedrin for murder. I stood before all of you a few months ago when I was sworn in as the first Greek State's Attorney in the history of Cook County, and I made a promise to pursue justice for the weak, the poor, the rich, and the powerful. For people of all shapes and sizes and stripes. It doesn't matter if you've been an angel before or a hardened criminal. If you are a victim of a crime in Cook County, my office will fight for you. I made the promise then, and I've never backtracked on it. It's set in stone."

Carpetopoulos had beads of sweat on the right side of his forehead, but the people in the break room didn't seem to notice. My hands twitched, and I knew it was only a matter of time before my eyelids followed suit. Stress is always undefeated.

"Lance Gedrin murdered Amy Pako. Plain and simple. It doesn't matter that he's a celebrity and he has all the high-powered lawyers money can buy. Murder is murder. Amy Pako was in her residency at Northwestern University trying to fulfill her lifelong dream of being a doctor. She lived to help others and always put a smile on their faces. She was top of her class and had millions of friends who adored her. She was a loving aunt and sister and daughter. Then Mr. Gedrin slit her throat and dumped her like a rotten piece of meat on I-57. The moment the appellate court vacated Mr. Gedrin's conviction on a technicality, I knew that our office was going to retry him. Justice never sleeps, and it will certainly not sleep for Amy Pako's family. I have been in contact with them throughout the day. They have expressed their deepest apologies that they couldn't be here today to witness this moment, but they have entrusted us with the very serious duty of fighting for Amy. We intend to do that with every ounce of strength and resolve in our bodies. I'll take some questions now."

The sharks were chomping at the bit.

"Does your intent to retry Mr. Gedrin have anything to do with the fact that his high- powered lawyer has gone missing? Sounds like a tactical advantage."

Carpetopoulos shook his head. "Listen. The fact that Mr. Gedrin's lawyer has gone missing is unfortunate. That matter is in the hands of the more than capable Chicago Police Department. They'll share any updates when they have them. But my office does not make decisions on pursuing criminal charges based on which lawyers are going to be in a courtroom. That's absolutely ridiculous. People who commit crimes need to be held accountable. Mr. Gedrin needs to be held accountable for his actions thirteen years ago. He went to prison, and rightly so, then was sprung on a technicality."

"Would you consider the constitution and its precedent a technicality?" another reporter asked.

"When you're convicted of murder based on both eyewitness testimony and a video confession and then it gets overturned because of *corpus delicti*, then yes, it's a technicality. Mr. Gedrin was very lucky on appeal. He escaped and he knows it. We had all the evidence we needed to put him away during the first trial. We had more than enough corroboration to prove the body of the crime. We firmly disagree with the appellate court, but there's nothing we can do about that now. Here we are. We're confident that the conviction will stick this time around, and a murderer won't be walking our streets anymore."

"What are the next steps in the court process?" asked yet another reporter.

"Now that we've stated our intent to retry Mr. Gedrin, we will be back in court tomorrow morning for an emergency status. Our office has already reached out to the law firm that's representing him in this matter. They'll continue to represent him. That's my understanding. Mr. Gedrin is already on bond pursuant to the appellate court order. But my office will readdress the matter of bond tomorrow, and we'll pick a new trial date."

Fuck.

"What timeframe are we looking at?" the same reporter asked.

"The sooner the better. Our office knows this case inside out, and the Pako family deserves to be heard in court as soon as possible. It's bad enough that your child is murdered, but when the killer walks free it's like she died all over again. We can't have that. No way. This new trial isn't going to drag on from our end. I can't speak for the defense though. You'd have to ask them what their plans are."

"Are you at all concerned that the jury pool will be tainted by those who used to watch all Mr. Gedrin's fights and steadfastly believe in his innocence?" The third reporter again.

"I don't want to jump the gun. Mr. Gedrin has the absolute right under the law to a trial of his choosing. He may very well opt for a bench trial. I don't know. If it does end up being a jury trial though, then of course there's concern that we may not be able to fill the jury box with those who will be completely sympathetic to our cause. But the same goes the other way, and I'm sure the defense will gripe that they wish they could have all their best jurors too. It's the nature of the beast. But listen, Mr. Gedrin hasn't been in a boxing ring for over thirteen years.

If not for a Snapchat of him shopping at the clearance rack he's really an afterthought till today."

"Is there any new evidence this time around that you think will be able to seal the deal?"

"I can't get into specifics because it's a pending case and I don't want any bar complaints. But I will say this. We are confident that we have all the evidence we need. You all were present for the first trial. We have all that evidence and more. We can prove this case not only beyond a reasonable doubt, but beyond *any* doubt."

Another reporter chimed in. "If you retry him and you get a hung jury, what then?"

This was the best question all day. I smiled. The sharks covered so many angles it'd give a mathematician a headache. And their facial expressions were priceless too.

"We have every intention to prove this case once and for all at this new trial," Carpetopoulos said. "We're not thinking of a third trial. We'll cross that bridge if it ever becomes an issue, but I don't like dealing in fiction. For now, we're all in on this prosecution."

"Who will be trying the case?"

"I will personally be trying this case with a few of my assistants. They're back up in the office prepping and didn't want to get bitten hard by all these questions."

The sharks laughed at the cheesy bit, and I hated them again.

"Do you have any words for Mr. Gedrin?" someone asked.

Carpetopoulos looked as though he'd been waiting for this question his whole life. It was a politician's wet dream. He looked straight into the camera.

"Nobody gets away with murder in my city," he said firmly. "All those titles and commercials and TV shows will mean absolutely nothing, Mr. Gedrin, once you go down for what you did. You can't box your way out of cold-blooded murder. Get ready for a knockout."

The sharks shouted a few more questions, but Carpetopoulos thanked them and left the podium. His army of robots followed him like they were on a string.

As I got up from my chair, it felt like a million eyes were on me. If I wasn't hungry like a hippo I would have stayed there and debated the whole case. I would have talked about all the highs and lows and all the nuances with anybody that would listen. Persistence is key.

But a cheeseburger is the best medicine sometimes. And considering there was a real possibility I'd be eating bologna sandwiches tomorrow, I needed to get out. I waited a minute for the room to clear. I could see I had some fans, but far more enemies.

Tempe left last. I said something to her, but don't remember what.

Tempe said nothing.

26

I cashed my advance at the nearest currency exchange. The guy at the front told me business was slow since most people did mobile deposits now. I asked him how to set it up on my phone and he said my phone was shitty and didn't have the right number of gigabytes. So much for the Jitterbug. As the guy counted out all the bills behind the glass I counted how many hours of freedom I had left. Judge make-a-name-for-himself would play to the cameras and change my bond. And I'd trade in my Macy's specials for a tan XL uniform.

Tempe didn't like tan.

"Here ya go, Mr. Gedrin," the guy said.

I expected a steady stream of vulgarities like I'd encountered on the way over. The news had struck a chord with random passersby. But this guy was cool.

"I appreciate it," I said.

"Get one of those shark lawyers. A Jewish one. My son had a drug charge and he hired Ezra Simpson. Loudmouth guy but my son beat the case. The state always thinks they have something, but when you challenge their asses they've got nothing."

I didn't reveal my complete trial strategy, but I did tell the guy that I didn't have a public pretender, and that satisfied him. I thanked him for his services and walked toward the lake. The reality was, Carpetopoulos was the latest suit in a long-ass line of suits trying to capitalize on my fame and misfortune. He worked his way up from traffic bullshit to drugs to murder, all the while aiming for the governor's mansion. Suits like him had the biggest egos in the world and could never quite temper it. The man was still in diapers when I kicked ass in the ring, but he thought he was the shit. As much as I wanted to jump through the screen and strangle him on live TV, I knew that Carpetopoulos would get his comeuppance eventually. The truth had no expiration date, and a trial was a no-holds-barred battle of wills. Under the biggest spotlight he'd fall back to obscurity.

And I'd get my title back. Everybody loved a good comeback story.

I crossed Adams and Michigan and passed the Art Institute. The lions said hello, and I said goodbye. I kept on toward the lake with no particular destination in mind. I knew I wouldn't get a lick of sleep if I tried to lie down now, but I figured delaying the inevitable might actually trick my body into submission. I crossed Columbus and debated whether to get that cheeseburger I'd fantasized about in the break room. I craved the grease, but I found I no longer had the appetite under the circumstances. Stress eating was no bueno. I sat down on some crooked steps and stared out at the boats docked on the water and the night runners training for the marathon next fall. Life was simple and beautiful on the outside if you gave it a chance.

My peace and solitude was broken by a group of graffiti

taggers who rolled up hooting and hollering and hugging each other. Somebody must have beat me to the complain-o-meter because a minute later cops on bikes chased them away. The taggers loved every minute of it, and for a moment I did too. Then I realized that those same asshole cops would testify against me soon. The blue wall lived on, and justice was the dirtiest word in town.

When I was perp-walked out of Sal's gym thirteen years ago, I never made peace with the world around me. I lived on a pedestal and never heard no for an answer. I took it all for granted and thought the case against me was a joke. A dream I'd wake up from and laugh about with my friends. Nobody would convict a celebrity. Especially a one-hundred-percent innocent one.

But life wasn't *Law & Order*.

Celebrities had baggage, and Amy Pako had a smile that melted your heart.

Judge Leroy Esteban set my initial bond at no bail. Mickey Jo, my "superstar" lawyer, told me I'd get out a few days later when he filed a motion to reduce bond. The case was assigned to Judge Norman Bishop. He denied the motion and I was remanded to the Cook County Jail—no bail. I sat and sat, and sat some more. I stared at the walls and did hundreds of pushups a day and listened to cons who told me that Judge Bishop was pretty fair. I debated whether to have a bench trial or a jury trial, and the committee of tan jumpsuits weighed in daily.

I opted for a jury trial.

No DNA.

No prints.

A shaky eyewitness.

And a bogus confession.

The jury would eat it up.

But what I didn't know, and would soon find out, was how fucked up juries could be. They see you in your suit and they know that you changed into it a few minutes before. They know you're some con who's trying to game them. And as much as they claim to not read the paper or know anything about you, they know you better than your steadiest girl. They see you beating the shit out of people on TV for a living and equate that with beating the shit out of people in real life. Jo wore wrinkled suits to trial and wore the same tie three days in a row. He gave me three sheets of legal paper to scribble my thoughts on, but he never once looked at them. He used all our peremptories during jury selection, and a few of our challenges for cause were sustained, but many were not. Meaning there were people on the jury who said they didn't think they could be fair, but after prodding from the judge said they would give it a shot. My life was on the line, and they would *give it a shot*. Wow. I wanted to knock all their asses out and show them that boxing carries over quite well outside the squared circle. But there were rules in a courtroom. It was a formal, sanctified place. Not a street fight. Obedience was real.

Jo put on a decent case.

The state put on a slightly less decent case.

I took the stand and gave my version of events. Which differed greatly from the state's version. But my version was completely accurate. I was in a bathtub filled with bubbles and chocolate getting an excellent goodbye present from a woman named Mindi. We were hanging out at the time, and she was going away to Italy for a few weeks. It was the best chocolate of my life.

But Mindi never came back to the States. Somebody got to her, and she refused to testify on my behalf.

And my alibi was fucked.

Closings were elaborate and showy. I tapped my foot to Jo's

arguments and squeezed the life out of my pencils for the state's. Jury instructions were read to the arbiters of my fate. They had a verdict in one hour and three minutes. Jo said quick verdicts favored the defense. I wholeheartedly agreed.

But the jury had other plans.

When the clerk read the verdict, my mind was honestly already on my next fight. Even though I'd been locked up for over a year pending trial, my team had lined up a bunch of title fights with the next Joe Schmoe young shit-talker trying to take my crown. Take your pick. The team thought the trial was a joke and the HBO execs did too, so they promised me a huge purse for an opponent of my choosing. Back from the joint to kick some ass. A la Tyson, but with better results. I signed on the dotted line after chow time.

Then the verdict was read.

GUILTY.

I missed it at first. It was the gasps in the courtroom that snapped me out of it. And then I saw Jo with his head down, and I heard the whispers, and I knew.

The contracts were ripped up. The team was disbanded. My title was stripped. I was officially a con. Public pretenders handled my appeals, which went nowhere. They were almost completely exhausted when I met Stevenson. She combed through thousands of hours of trial transcripts. And when she found nothing, she took another look. And another. On the fourth full read-through she realized that one of the most basic legal doctrines could spring me. It was almost too good to be true. *Corpus delicti.* The body of the crime. The state needed some independent corroboration, aside from my alleged confession, that a murder had occurred. The eyewitness was so shaky, and that, coupled with the lack of DNA and prints, wasn't enough corroboration.

Carpetopoulos called it a technicality.

I called it poetry in motion. The law flexing its muscles. Too bad the law and actual innocence never make good dinner mates, though. I'd be put through the wringer again.

Carpetopoulos was going for a knockout.

But so was I.

A fighter never quits.

27

My tenure at the shittiest motel in the shittiest part of downtown came to an end later that night. Not because I was riding high with my advance or because I was moving on to my latest adventure, but because my motel room window had been shattered to pieces and had yellow caution tape all over it. Black marker lined every inch of my door with gargantuan displays of phallic imagery. I laughed at the vandals' creative touch and vowed to analyze the designs for future reference. And in the parking lot, a group of gawkers was taking pictures.

I wasn't a stickler for square footage, and would have gladly moved rooms if it meant a similar window view minus the carnage. But the sign out front, which had all bulbs intact now, clearly stated "No Vacancies." Damn.

I went to my room. The window was one thing; my valuables were another. I didn't have much, but my backpack and stray bags were my casa. My livelihood depended on keeping these few worldly possessions. I checked under the bed and felt around two times before I finally pulled everything out. Still there. Muy bueno.

I went to the bathroom and checked the shower stall. My shampoo was still there too. The vandals seemed like reasonable folk who'd lost their cool in the moment. After examining the rest of the room, I concluded that whoever messed with my window hadn't been trying to put me in the grave next to Stine. Those hombres shot first and asked questions later. These vandals were small potatoes, and the broken window reeked of amateur hour. For one, half the window was still intact in one of the corners, and the brick used for the nefarious deed was tiny. The geniuses couldn't even bring the right tools for the job.

The keeper showed up to deliver more bad news.

"You can't stay here anymore," he said. "I can't have drama like this. I don't know who the fuck you pissed off, but somebody found out you're here and is trying to send a message. And that message is gonna make my insurance go through the roof, man."

"I need another look at your lost and found," I said. I wanted to find another dress shirt for the road.

"Why?"

"I left a smaller, blue dress shirt."

"There are no shirts, man." The keeper was annoyed and operating on frequently interrupted sleep.

"I need the box."

The keeper frowned. "You have till morning. Then you're gone. No excitement, please."

"What if I wanna jam out on an acoustic guitar?"

"Don't push it."

As the keeper left, I wondered if I'd heed his advice. I was leaning yes. I was exhausted, and I had a big day ahead of me.

I packed all my things into my backpack and looked around

the room for any bells and whistles I had forgotten. When I looked outside, the gawkers had moved on, but had been replaced by two detectives in jeans, nice dress shirts, and combat boots. They scribbled in their notepads and took pictures of the damage. When their eyes met mine through the caution tape, they smiled. A *gotcha* smile. A *you're going back in, asshole* smile. They wouldn't go easy for my trial. They'd pack the gallery.

The wind blew fiercely through the open window, and getting any shuteye was a pipe dream. But if I survived the last twelve years I'd survive the night. I closed my eyes and I heard the birds and the owls and some canines and felines not on the same page.

Then my phone buzzed.

Tempe.

I flipped it open and couldn't hear anything. I was regressing. Two minutes later I found she'd sent me a text message. I had no idea how to send one back, but I could receive them. Tempe didn't hate me after all.

Hang in there, she'd written. Followed by a smiley face.

Easier said than done when the weight of the world is on your shoulders and you're one breath away from isolation and servitude. But I had a fresh pair of suits now, so maybe it would be different.

I wanted to send her some witty picture, but I was still expanding my technological acumen. In less than a week I'd gone from bars to a potato museum to diners to a Jitterbug. I pulled out the phone manual and figured it out. Now I just had to figure out what to write. Texts were a whole other ballgame. I sat there thinking of clever lines, and nothing came to me. Life was complicated sometimes.

I kept it simple. "Gracias."

Followed by a smiley face.

Tempe and her crew had their work cut out for them.

28

I woke up at three a.m. and couldn't go back to sleep. My body knew the score. I did two hundred pushups, seventy-three crunches, and twelve burpees. Then I showered and picked the best ensemble for the occasion. It was a battle of epic proportions. In one corner, the keeper's shirt from the lost and found. In the other corner, an olive-green muscle tee that I'd picked up during my travels. Two wrinkles, but swaggy. I made a split-second decision and chose the tee. The bottoms were a piece of cake. The infamous clearance-rack jeans. The shoes took a little more concentration. I hemmed and hawed for bit, then went with Chelsea boots again. I was in business. I packed the dress shirt away and put my backpack on. I looked like a suave expeditioner. I took one last look at the room and pitied the next tenant. The caution tape had peeled off the window, and the sticky summer air said hello.

I checked out with the keeper. He bid me safe travels and gave me a couple mints for the inconvenience of displacing me from the Ritz. I asked for three more mints for the road and the keeper obliged. First thing I did after that was find a McDonald's. A big day meant a big breakfast of champions. I had coffee, an apple pie, a McGriddle, one hash brown, and a small cup of OJ. Sal would be proud.

I had an hour till court. I knew Tempe would already be at the courthouse, prepping the case. She'd sent me some texts last night going into strategy, but I ignored them. Lawyers needed to lawyer and clients needed to make insane demands while trying to stay the hell out of the legal morass. I'd say my piece if and when it was absolutely necessary.

It took me three buses to get to the courthouse. I sat all the way in back each time, and surprisingly nobody came up to me. The last bus dropped me right in front of the courthouse at 8:42. Court started at nine on the dot. Half the bus got off with me and shuffled up the courthouse steps. Now I understood why they were so quiet. No point in jabbering with somebody when you're fighting your own case and might get fucked. 'Twas the way of the world.

I saw the sharks a mile away. They were waiting near the revolving doors that led inside. Last time, I never had the pleasure of going through them each day, since I was no bail. But this time I couldn't avoid them. At least for today.

The courthouse had gone through a name change a few years back, and was now called the Leighton Criminal Courthouse. It was nestled in the heart of the west side of Chicago, and its huge monolithic structure and Roman lettering on the top facade of the building screamed history and justice. The locals all called it 26th Street, and since I'd once been a local at the jail, that name had stuck with me too.

When I came up the steps, the sharks had a feeding frenzy. Ten cameras flashed, and it seemed like twenty mics took their place. Everybody shouted, but I kept moving. They all asked the same questions that called for the same answers. Answers they knew beforehand, but asked anyway. They wanted the soundbite of the century, but they came up empty. They did get a nice visual though. One of the cameras tested me by blocking the revolving door, and I swatted it away like I did that kid from the tattoo shop. I smiled and kept going. I knew that would make all the headlines, but when my ingress was blocked I had no choice.

As I stepped out of the revolving door I found myself packed in a tight line with all the other excellent citizens of Cook County. We were like cattle for the slaughter, shuffling an inch at a time as the brave ones all the way in front did the honors and removed their belts, metals, and other valuables. When it was my turn, the deputies smirked. I followed their commands and took out my phone, wallet, and belt. I gave them my backpack. They made me take off my shoes and socks, which nobody else in line had to do. The assholes were loving every minute of it.

"Have a good day, sir," one of the deputies said.

"Where can I get a fat cheeseburger?" I said.

The deputy turned red, but before he could get his revenge I got my things from the conveyer belt and trudged on.

I took a right past security and was stopped by another deputy near some makeshift lockers. He told me cell phones were prohibited in the courthouse, except for authorized personnel—which meant people like Tempe. They could twitter and make chats snap all day, but us common folk had to follow the rules. Either leave the phone at home or entrust the county to house it while your fate is being decided by the judge. Hence the lockers. They used to be outside the security checkpoint, but after a bunch of defendants came late to court and got a shit ton of warrants, practices were modified. The lockers now stood past security, but latecomers couldn't save a warrant either way. Judges didn't care about the nitty-gritty of technological safekeeping.

I gave my phone to the deputy, and he looked it over like it had a hidden bomb in it. He was on the same wavelength as the smirkers manning the security line.

"No iPhone, boxer man?" the deputy said.

"Fruit makes me nauseous," I said.

The deputy stared daggers at me, but he didn't take it any further. I parted with the Jitterbug but made sure to tell her I'd be back. I didn't make any other promises. With my luck, I wouldn't be taken back into custody, but my phone would be lost and in somebody else's custody.

I walked down the hallway, took a right, then a left, and walked down a hallway with rustic pictures of the courthouse on the ceiling. They didn't evoke any beauty at all, and I doubted that the hundreds of people who passed through on a daily basis would disagree. My case was assigned to room 504, the very same courtroom in which they'd filmed *Presumed Innocent*. It also happened to be one of the larger courtrooms, since the lower levels were mainly fishbowl-style courtrooms with glass partitions separating the gallery from court personnel. But my case was big-time, and big-time cases deserved big-time spaces.

I fully expected a shark attack, a gallery packed to the rafters, and a multitude of defendants who had court that day and wouldn't be so fortunate as to proceed after me. Right after my case was dealt with some of the sharks would stick around and the judge would make a point of demonstrating that he treated all defendants the same. Which meant they'd be screwed over in the name of Lady Justice too.

The elevator up was a tight squeeze. A few reporters scribbled in their notepads and looked at me out of the corner of their eyes. One of the beauties of the Cook County court system is that unlike the rest of the world, cameras are prohibited in the actual courtroom, unless approved beforehand. Practically speaking, this means that run-of-the-mill status dates are not on camera, but super high-profile matters are. I expected my case to be on camera, but not until the actual trial. I was hopeful that today would bring only scribblers and sketch artists only. Videographers no bueno.

The ride up took forever. People got off on two, three, and four. What should have been a twenty-second elevator ride took two minutes easy. But when I got out, it was all worth it. Tempe was waiting for me, briefcase in hand, dressed in a new suit. She was smoking hot, and I wanted to rip her clothes off like last night.

She gave me a sly smile. "You clean up well, champ. And thanks for the strategy session."

I returned her smile. "Ditto."

We stepped down the hall to our courtroom, but instead of going inside, Tempe led me to the grimy window that overlooked the Cook County Jail.

"We've got time," she said. "Let them get situated. We'll be the first on the call anyway."

"Can't wait." I looked out the window, taking note of how peaceful the bars looked on the outside. But I knew the inside was death.

"How much sleep did you get?" Tempe asked.

"Two hours and ten minutes."

"Same. I always get nervous when I go to court on big stuff."

"It's just a bond hearing. And picking a trial date. You lawyers blow everything up. Five minutes tops."

"You could go back into custody." Tempe's eyes found mine. I wished they could stay there till I told them not to.

"Not my first rodeo. I'll be cool."

"I don't want you to be cool. I want you with me. If you go in, you'll never come out."

She took my hand. The sparks were still there, and then some. The jolts of electricity that went up my spine were a million times stronger and my chest tingled thanks. I rubbed the outside of her hand until she broke away and looked out the window again.

"If you beat this case you'll make partner," I said. "Or you go on your own and you'll be the next Gertrude Stevenson."

She laughed. "Nobody wants to be the next Gertrude. That's old news. They want the next Tempe. I'm my own woman. My own lawyer. She's long gone."

"Don't say that."

"If you're expecting her to come waltzing through those doors to win your case, check yourself."

"I only have one attorney fighting for me?" I said, teasing. "Shame."

"The partners don't wanna touch this case. Maybe one will sit at counsel table with us for now. But if this goes to trial and they don't end up tossing it, I'll assemble a team, trust me.

"A dream team?"

"Yeah."

"Get Johnnie Cochran."

"He's dead."

"Get Barry Scheck then."

"He's in New York and he's not interested."

I asked about the rest of the OJ lawyers, and Tempe shook her head. No. The firm wasn't going to tag-team a case with an attorney from out of state who carried not only a ton of baggage, but had no knowledge of the local court rules. The dream team Tempe had in mind would be local attorneys, and I didn't know any more names so I couldn't contribute. And when Tempe used the words *pro hac vice*, and I lost focus.

"Ask for house arrest," I said.

"That's stupid. You can't go anywhere. You don't have a valid Cook County address and you'll be cooped inside all day. You'd only get movement for court or attorney visits."

"I don't mind attorney visits," I said with a smile.

Tempe punched me in the shoulder. "It's more trouble than it's worth. Trust me."

"But I get all this credit. If we drag the case out for a couple years and things are looking like shit I can cop a deal and I'll have served all the time. I'd be out."

"You're an awesome jailhouse lawyer. But no. We're asking to keep the bond as is."

I was cool with that. I was on an I-Bond, which meant that I was released on my own signature. Just show up on time to all court dates until the case is resolved. Simple as that. If the judge kept it, I'd be golden. It'd give me ample time to fight my case and investigate others. Stevenson. Stine. I'd come to this great city for a reason.

"Or I can give up my advance," I said. "I can post that."

Tempe smiled. "But you worked so hard for it."

We laughed, and our eyes met again. Tempe was special, and I hoped I'd be able to spend a lot more time with her to remind her of that.

I wanted to give her a good-luck kiss before we went in, but Carpetopoulos spoiled the party. He came past wheeling a big squeaky cart with a shitload of files on it. He was flanked by three suits, one of whom held the courtroom door open. Before he went in, Carpetopoulos turned to me and said, "Good morning, Mr. Gedrin."

He completely ignored Tempe, and then was gone.

29

J udge Stanley Romero would decide my fate. He wore orange spectacles and an orange tie. His hair was in a ponytail and his teeth were blindingly white. He came out at 9:03 and joked around with the deputies for a couple minutes before calling cases. I sat in the middle row on the right side of the courtroom next to a young Hispanic couple who'd decided it was a great idea to bring an infant to court. Judges could see through that ploy in a heartbeat and didn't give a shit. I wanted to warn them, but they were sitting next to an annoying blogger who'd have a field day if he heard my advice. Tempe was up front in the well of the courtroom with a bunch of other attorneys.

Then Judge Romero said, "Nixon Bates."

The media was confused, but I wasn't. Judges called whatever cases they wanted in whatever order they wanted. When they had a media case, most judges wanted the masses out of their courtroom as quickly as possible, so they called it first. But this was Romero's court and Romero's rules. I could be called next, or I could be called last. I had nothing but time on my hands. And a backpack that I would entrust to the Hispanic couple when it was my turn.

An old black man in a cane walked slowly up to the bench, along with his attorney, who beat him in terms of years of service and had a cane of his own.

"Your Honor, for the record, Jason Nederich, N-E-D-E-R-I-C-H on behalf of Mr. Bates. Judge, we're here today—"

"I know why we're here today, counsel," Romero said. "Your client didn't show up to court last time and I issued a warrant. You advanced the case to today, presumably because your client has come to his senses and wants me to quash and recall the warrant, correct?"

The old attorney had the wind taken out of his sails. I didn't know much about Romero, but I knew enough to realize that things weren't going well to start the day. There were murmurs from the shark section of the gallery.

The old attorney said, "Yes, Your Honor—"

"Why weren't you in court, Mr. Bates?" Romero lowered his spectacles to the bridge of his nose and furrowed his brow.

"I mixed up the court date, sir. I went to Daley Center for my other case, and they said I didn't have no court, and I realized I was supposed to be at 26th."

Romero shook his head. "You missed court because you have another case? What kind of case is it?"

"A DUI, Your Honor."

Bates looked pathetic, but then again who didn't in the criminal lack-of-justice system? The door creaked behind me, and more people piled in. The courtroom had ten rows on each side, and eight of them were filled. In another couple minutes I expected full capacity. The Hispanic couple next to me held hands tightly.

"Were there any injuries?" Romero asked.

The old attorney tried to save the day. "Judge—"

"Quiet, counselor."

Bates nodded. "Yes, Your Honor. I went to the hospital, and she did too. She got out next day or two. Nothing big."

Romero looked Bates up and down and then said the magic words. "Warrant executed."

The deputies were ready. They'd been standing behind Bates from the moment his name was called, and now they took him into custody. Off the floor and into the back. The attorney shook his head. Bates said nothing. If anybody in the gallery wasn't paying attention before, they were bolt upright in their seats and weren't saying shit now.

I stayed calm. If there's anything I've learned being in court, it's that judges swing like the wind, literally one second to the next. Bates's misery could be my gain. Hopefully.

Romero took out another file. "Katie Seton," he said.

It was shaping up to be a long day.

A thirty-something white woman with a nose ring appeared at the bench with no attorney.

"Ms. Seton, you've been charged with two counts of identity theft. Do you have a lawyer, ma'am?"

Seton was shaking. "No, no. I can't afford one."

"*How much do you make?*" Romero snapped.

She answered quickly. "Two thousand a month."

"Do you have any dependents?"

"I'm not dependent on nobody."

Romero was frustrated, and so was I. The lady clearly qualified for a public pretender, but Romero was going through the whole rigamarole of determining her assets and liabilities.

"I didn't ask you if you are dependent on anyone," Romero said. "Listen when I'm talking to you or you'll go into custody too. We have plenty of space back there. *Do you claim anybody on your taxes as a dependent, other than yourself?*"

"No," Seton said.

"Okay. Do you pay rent?"

"Yes. Nine hundred a month."

"Do you have children?"

"Yes. One boy."

Romero smiled. "So you do have a dependent."

"Umm...yes. I'm sorry."

"Public defender appointed. Ma'am, have a seat and somebody will come talk to you."

Romero handed the file to the clerk, who in turn handed it to one of the public pretenders who walked up.

I looked over to the defense table, and while all the other waiting lawyers were bullshitting and cracking jokes under their breath, Tempe was all business, examining her notes. She'd make a hell of a lawyer someday if she left the firm. Carpetopoulos was glued to his phone, smiling. I couldn't tell if it was an apple or some other fruit.

Romero grabbed another file. "Lance Gedrin."

All eyes on me. The sharks started scribbling, the gallery was transfixed, the lawyers from all sides were pointing and whispering. If I tripped on the way to the bench, TMZ would make millions. I left my backpack with the Hispanic couple and walked the red carpet.

Tempe was already at the bench. I stood to her left. Carpetopoulos stood far right, flanked by his cronies. Behind me three deputies formed a U, as if I could escape with all the world watching. I'd need better shoes for that. Chelseas weren't made for speed.

Romero said, "Nice to see you again, Mr. Carpetopoulos. Glad the high post isn't keeping you from trying cases in my courtroom."

Carpetopoulos smiled widely. "No, Your Honor. Very glad to be here."

I wanted to punch him, but Romero would find me in contempt.

"Judge," Tempe said, "for the record, Kayla Tempe on behalf of Mr. Gedrin. We're here on a remand from the first district. The state has filed an emergency motion."

Romero waved Tempe off, and she stopped. He was nicer to her than he was to the old attorney earlier, but probably only because Tempe was hot. The judge opened my file, sifted through some papers, then put them back.

He looked to Carpetopoulos. "State."

"Judge the first district remanded as counsel aptly stated. Our office was instructed to determine whether or not we would proceed against Mr. Gedrin. Our office reviewed everything as quick as we could, being cognizant of the fact that we have a young victim and her family who so desperately want closure in this matter. We've made the decision to retry Mr. Gedrin for the murder of Amy Pako, and we'd like to address the issue of bond." He puffed his chest out. He'd never seen a bench press in his life.

Romero shook his head. "Mr. Gedrin was already given an I-Bond. He's presumed innocent. I understand this is a high-profile matter, but every defendant is entitled to the presumption of innocence. Counsel."

Tempe said, "That's correct, Your Honor. Mr. Gedrin is cloaked in the presumption of innocence. He has maintained his innocence from day one. I'm not going to try the case here, but I will say the case against Mr. Gedrin had no DNA. No prints. A shaky eyewitness—"

"And a video confession," Romero said.

"Which we submit was coerced from the get-go. The officers were fact-feeding Mr. Gedrin, and all the details of the crime were given to him in the interview room. He didn't volunteer any of it."

Tempe was killing it, and I was enjoying every minute. When Romero looked over at me I tried to hide my smirk.

"What troubles me," the judge said, "is the fact that we have an admission. I understand you contend it wasn't voluntary, but that's something that should be taken up in a motion. In any event on its face we have an admission, there's no alibi, and it was raining the night of the murder, washing away any forensic component."

"Judge—"

"Let me finish, Ms. Tempe. Couple all that with the fact that Mr. Gedrin by profession knocks people around and renders them comatose, he certainly had the means to commit this crime. Furthermore, testimony at the original trial made clear that he got into an argument at a strip club and made threats hours before the murder. I'm quite familiar with the file. Ms. Tempe...your client has his hand up."

Court was all about decorum. I knew the rules. You couldn't blurt things out and risk being berated and taken off the floor. Besides, judges didn't appreciate being talked over. It was an ego thing more than anything else. So I had my hand up, waiting patiently to say my piece. Carpetopoulos wouldn't know what hit him.

Neither would Tempe.

She whispered in my ear. "What are you doing? Let me handle this."

I whispered back. "Let me speak. I have a right to speak. Please."

Tempe clenched her jaw and turned toward the bench. "Judge, my client would like to address the court. This is against advice at this time."

Romero took his glasses completely off. "Mr. Gedrin you do understand that your attorney is advising you not to say anything? And that anything you say can and will be used against you? The court reporter is taking all of this down."

"Yes, Your Honor. But I want to say my piece."

Romero leaned back in his chair. I could tell he wanted to explode, but with the sharks watching he wanted to avoid the news articles about his lack of impartiality even more. After a long pause, he sighed. "Very well, Mr. Gedrin."

I took a step forward, and the deputies did too. Then I took Carpetopoulos to school. Just like I had planned it.

"Judge, I'm completely innocent of these bogus charges. Then and now. I'm not running away from anybody. I'll be at all my court dates on time and ready to go. I'm demanding trial, right now."

Carpetopoulos looked like he was going to have a heart attack. Tempe too.

Carpetopoulos protested. "Judge, this is a murder case! We can't go to trial just like that. There are witnesses, exhibits—"

Romero said, "Mr. Gedrin, your attorney would be the one demanding trial. And since she hasn't filed a written demand on your behalf, it doesn't seem like she wants to proceed that way. For strategy reasons. Attorneys control the strategy, defendants control whether or not to go trial, plead, testify, appeal, that sort of thing. Understand?"

I understood all of this. I was the Professor. Which led into the next part of my plan—the part that would school Tempe. Things would never be the same again, but I had no other choice.

"Judge," I said. "I want to go *pro se*. I don't want a lawyer anymore. I'm demanding trial."

The courtroom gasped. People were eating it up.

Romero banged his gavel and everybody quieted down.

"Mr. Gedrin! Do you think this is some sort of circus?" he said. "You want to represent yourself? What kind of training do you have? You were in custody for twelve years before a lawyer got you out, remember? A lawyer at the very firm that Ms. Tempe is with now. Mr. Gedrin a client who acts as his own lawyer has a fool for a client."

I knew I'd get backlash. But I also knew that if I was going to succeed, I had to stay firm.

Tempe looked over at me with eyes that seemed to say *What the fuck are you doing?* If we weren't in court she'd strangle the shit out of me. No second date.

"I understand the risks, Your Honor. I want to go *pro se*. I'm demanding trial."

Romero put his glasses back on and squeezed the life out of his temples. He read me the *pro se* admonishments, basically the required rights that I need to be informed of when going *pro se*, things like I have to follow the rules of evidence, I won't be given special treatment, et cetera. It took a few minutes, and when he was done, Romero looked me in the eye.

"Mr. Gedrin. Having received all these admonishments, do you still wish to go pro se?"

"Yes," I said.

Romero shook his head and looked over at Tempe. "Attorney Kayla Tempe is given leave to withdraw. Thank you for your work on this case, counsel."

Tempe stared a million bullets at me, then walked back to the defense table and sat down. The other attorneys in the courtroom whispered things to her, but her eyes were on me and the shit show that would follow.

It was now me and Carpetopoulos. *Mano a Mano.* The deputies closed the gap on my right though, so I couldn't get a clean punch in even if I tried.

Romero gathered himself. "Once a defendant demands trial," he said, "the state has one hundred sixty days to bring the defendant to trial if he's out of custody. One hundred twenty days if he's in. But this case has been tried before. The victim's family needs closure, and I imagine that Mr. Gedrin does too. While I still think he's making a big mistake representing himself with no sort of trial experience, it's his right. And he's been admonished. These are the cards we have on the table. This trial is going in two days. My schedule is clear."

"Judge!" Carpetopoulos practically shrieked. He looked like he wanted to climb the bench. "We can't have everybody here in two days! We're gonna have to commence and continue it."

"No way, counsel. Have everybody here or a continuance will be denied. We're not going to have a case from the last millennium on my docket. You're the state's attorney for this whole county. Not a line attorney. I'm sure you can work your magic and have everything good to go."

"What about the issue of bond?" Carpetopoulos said.

"Ah, yes. Bond will stand. Mr. Gedrin, if you lose this trial, you're going into custody faster than I can say WBO. Got that?"

"Yes, Your Honor."

Romero wrote something on the file. "Great. That's it." He picked up the next file. "Edmond Villa."

I went back to my seat and picked up my backpack. When I looked back at the defense table, Tempe was gone.

30

Instead of getting the hell out of Dodge, I hung a right and found the men's bathroom. The combo of my breakfast of champions and Romero's last-minute ruling made me wanna piss a fountain. I pushed open the door and found both stalls occupied. It was a small space, so I waited outside. Down the hall I noticed the deputies going in and out of the courtroom through a separate door, with a couple of judges following suit. The attorneys had their own special door as well, left of the courtroom. Tempe must have used it after my case was over. I wanted to sit down and explain everything in detail, but I didn't have my phone. Maybe we'd do brunch.

Romero had come through for me, but now was when things would get interesting. Carpetopoulos had shit his pants when I schooled him, but things were usually overblown in a courtroom, and he'd recover. With all the state's resources at his disposal, he'd have all his witnesses lined up by tomorrow morning, and in two days they'd be smiling single file in front of Romero. The state wouldn't risk the case getting tossed because of scheduling difficulties. Carpetopoulos wanted that governor's mansion more than I wanted my freedom, and he'd do anything to get it.

The bathroom door opened and a little kid ran out to rejoin his parents. I wasn't in a rush to be a piece of cattle again, so I waited some more to have the bathroom all to myself. Foot traffic was light here; the far end of the hallway looked like it was reserved for authorized personnel, so maybe that had something to do with it. I leaned against the wall and wondered where I'd next find lodging. My advance wasn't in danger of running out anytime soon, but I wasn't going to be careless with it either. Life was filled with surprises. Maybe I'd find a two-star hotel for a night, or settle for a motel opposite my old one to taunt the keeper who'd banished me. Options were muy bueno.

The door opened again and a man in a Cubs cap walked out. I went in and hummed a tune as I took a piss. When I didn't have a deputy staring me down or somebody waiting to shank me, I went with Queen or the latest rap compilation. It wasn't close this time. I went with "We Are the Champions." A minute later I cut the song short and washed my hands.

And that's when everything changed.

The mirror was blood red.

With a message on it.

For one person, and one person only.

Me.

"The reporter should have kept her mouth shut."

I ran out of the bathroom, looking both ways for my quarry. But the guy in the Cubs cap had a two-minute head start. The throngs of people in the main hallway were gone. The sharks too. The elevators were on other floors. I checked the stairs, and didn't hear any steps below. I ran across the hall and checked the other set of stairs. Nada. There were four courtrooms on the hall, and three of them weren't even in session. I checked the locks to make sure.

That left only 504. Romero's court.

Before I could open the door, the Hispanic couple from earlier came out and smiled. The Hispanic guy said, "Go get 'em man. Like you did Ed Davis."

I smiled. I'd knocked Davis's ass outside the ring and onto the judges' table in twenty seconds flat. Those were the days.

After the couple shuffled off, I opened the door to 504 and peered inside. Romero was lecturing some gangbanger about dropping dirty. I scanned the gallery and came up empty. A deputy spotted me and motioned for me to come inside the courtroom and sit, but I closed the door.

The hallway was empty. I pushed the button for the elevators, and when I turned around I ran into Tempe, texting on her phone.

"Not one word," she said.

The elevator came and she got on. She didn't hold the door, and I wasn't about to test the stopping mechanism of the county elevators. As the doors closed, Tempe remained glued to her phone.

I hit the button again.

And this time I bumped into the partner who'd introduced me to the rest of the firm. He wore a suit that looked like a million bucks, and he had one of those fancy brown briefcases. He'd made it to my hearing after all. He was late to the party, but better late than never I guess.

"We had a great day," I said.

"You're fired," the partner said. "Conflict of interest. You understand. Drop off your ID and we'll deal with the advance later."

"I'll fight you for it."

I held his gaze, and I could see the partner was scared shitless.

When the elevator came back again, I decided to do the

gentlemanly thing and let the partner take it down solo. He pressed the close-door button so hard the circuitry of the building should have complained.

Three minutes later, I grabbed the next elevator. I took the same hallways and passed the same pictures on the ceilings. I gave my ticket to the deputy and got my phone back. It looked fine, but the battery was out.

The sharks were still waiting outside, and I sidestepped them like a boss. There wasn't a bus in sight, so I settled for a cab. I looked out my window for the Cubs fan and came up empty.

31

The motel opposite the keeper who banished me also had no vacancies, so I found a Comfort Inn a few blocks away. There was a yellow neon sign, a gumball machine, a stuffed animal depository, and a green yoyo in front. I wanted to be one step ahead of the gawkers at all times, so I paid cash for one night only. The new keeper and old keeper couldn't collude even if they tried.

My room was smaller than my old one, but cleaner. The bed smelled like lilacs and the carpeting didn't have any pet dander or foreign fluids. The bathroom had half a bar of soap on the sill, but a fresh package next to it. It took me a couple hours to charge my phone, but when everything lit up again all was quiet. No calls from Tempe. No texts. No voicemails. She was off the grid and I had no idea if she'd ever come back. It'd been a few hours since court wrapped up, and she was probably prepping for another deposition or taking shit from the rest of the partners. I fully expected her to hold her own and have a retort for everything. The more people pushed, the more she pushed back. I loved that about her. She didn't kowtow to anybody, and I wanted her in my corner. She fought hard for me at the bench and at times she reminded me of a younger Gertrude Stevenson going up against the world. But I still felt bad about double-crossing her. And the more time that passed without hearing from her, the more I felt a void inside. A ship without its stern. A soldier without a gun. Henri without a leash. The partner could stop my checks, but he couldn't stop me from wanting Tempe. No way, hombre.

On the positive side, the Comfort Inn lived up to its billing. The TV had twelve more channels than my former abode, with a wide selection of movies, TV shows, infomercials, scantily clad coeds making dreams come true, and news. I liked the ice cream scooper and meat thermometer products so much that I vowed to set aside some money for them. If the partner tried super hard to collect my advance, I'd part with the scooper in lieu of cash.

The news was awesome. I flipped to one of the local stations, and sure enough my antics from earlier had whetted the sharks' appetite. They dubbed me the *"pro se* punisher," and they questioned whether or not Carpetopoulos would be ready for the showdown in a couple days. The talking heads went back and forth on whether I could beat the case with no experience. The consensus was no, but the consensus was also that my case was stranger than fiction. Anything could happen. Damned right. The segment hopped back and forth between the studio and the reporters live from 26th Street. I scanned the background for the Cubs fan again but again came up empty. He could run, but he couldn't hide. Sooner or later our paths would cross. He wanted me, and I wanted him. And when I found him, it wouldn't be pretty. To the victor go the spoils.

After five more minutes of watching the same loop of shots, I called it quits and shut off the TV. I remembered that while the partner wanted me to drop off my ID, there was something he *didn't* ask me for at all.

Something he probably wanted, but wouldn't get.

Vegas's file.

It was still in my possession, and I had every intention of keeping it till I got answers.

I opened my backpack and tossed the file onto the bed. The gun shop in Kentucky was a dead end. So was the park. And so was the Pink Purse. But every door that closed meant that somewhere another one opened. Pointing the way. If I kept looking, I'd find it.

I took the papers out of the file, one by one. For a moment I thought maybe I'd find some reference to the Cubs fan, but I knew that was too good to be true. All I knew about him was that he wore a cap and was shorter than me.

So I started at the very beginning. The indictment. The police reports. The investigator notes. Stevenson had kept a good file, despite the coffee stains on some of the pages. I leafed through it all, slowly, methodically. An hour later, I'd reached the last page of the file and had come up with a bunch of nada. So much for my investigative skills. Maybe Romero was right: I rendered people comatose by profession. That's who I was. A bruiser. I couldn't cut it out here in the real world. The nine-to-five morning commuter crowd. I was an athlete. A fighter. A champion. I was the annoying asshole who came from modest means and rose to the top, had a taste of glory and the high life and all the trappings of success before the fall.

Nothing compared to that high, and I craved it like a junkie craved the next hit. I was a killer.

I stretched my neck, and the headache I was getting left in a heartbeat. I wanted a nap, but it was useless. It was half past one. I was too wired to sleep. I needed to pass the time. Tempe wasn't coming, so I needed something else.

I picked up the Vegas file one last time. I told myself that if I didn't find anything, I'd grab a nice turkey club and go to the zoo. The sun was out, and admission was one hundred percent gratis.

Something drew me back to the supplemental reports. Maybe it was the fact that they had double the narrative section on them compared to the rest of the file, or the fact that there were more officer entries on them. I scanned the lines again, looking at the fine print under the officers' signatures. There were times and dates and small boxes with computer readouts. The Pink Purse address was there, along with a bunch of redacted portions deemed too provocative for Stevenson. Which was stupid. Attorneys had an ethical duty to keep discovery in their possession and not encourage any client criminal conduct. The fact that CPD felt that Stevenson couldn't be trusted was a slap in the face.

When Vegas got popped, seven officers busted up his card game. Vegas and his Serbian cronies had made quite the impression. I went over the same names and the same DOBs, and the same alleged admissions that were made on scene. The cronies all used the Pink Purse address and were clearly skilled in the art of denial and bullshit. Since Vegas had them on payroll, the officers couldn't put additional obstructing charges on them. The Zemun was a brotherhood, and Vegas called all the shots from both near and far. Sandy was right on the money.

I kept looking.

And on page four of the supplemental report, I found it.

The narrative of the poker game was five whole paragraphs and about one page and a half, followed by post-custody actions. After all the officers arrived on scene they busted up the poker game within seconds. No licenses. No paperwork. No prescriptions for the drugs. Vegas was taken into custody along with the rest. Presumed innocent until proven guilty. But that wasn't the point.

Under the custodial comments section, the lockup keepers back at the county jail had a duty to input any important information that related to a detainee. Things like mental health diagnoses or medical problems or important medications or whether or not this was a first-time arrest or a high-profile case. More than anything, this was a way for the lockup personnel to cover their asses in case one of the defendants was in a litigating mood in civil court. Nothing teaches effective note-taking better than a multi-million-dollar handout.

Vegas had no issues worth noting.

But one of the cronies did.

The line read "M/1 first-time arrest...family in Goose Island has inhaler." Underneath was an address.

I smiled. It could be nothing. But it could be everything.

I scribbled the address down on one of the Comfort Inn complimentary stationery pads. My investigative skills were back in business. My confidence was sky-high.

And this time I wasn't on the clock.

32

Thirteen minutes later I was on a CTA train for the first time in twenty years. The grimy floor, windows, and ads hadn't changed one bit. The odors either. I sat in the rear-most car on the right-hand side in the lone seat that faced a utility box, while the others faced the direction of travel. My destination was three stops away, making an Uber obsolete under the circumstances. A cab was a similar waste of time and resources. I stared out the window at the afternoon commuters invading the city. They were an eclectic mix of students, young professionals, hipsters, punks, and other creatives who didn't believe in linear eight-hour shifts. I couldn't quite peg the exact ratio of haves and have-nots, but bottom line, diversity reigned supreme and brought character in such a large metropolis.

The address in Vegas's file was in the heart of Goose Island. Known for its burgeoning factories and warehouses, the neighborhood was on the outskirts of downtown Chicago. It wasn't exactly a tourist hotbed, but it was something. A step in the right direction. A wheel in the administration of justice. A kernel in the corn.

Maybe Vegas was there with his Serbian cronies.

Or somebody else on my hit list.

I'd be ready no matter what. Without Tempe's assistance. While my sleuthing was on the rise again without any formal employment, Tempe and I were back at square one. Being complete strangers. Being cold. It had been close to six hours since the elevator doors closed in my face and Tempe made no effort to stop them. Granted, she probably didn't want to sacrifice a limb to test the county structures any more than I did, but a picture spoke a thousand words. She was working through things, and that was cool. But even if she came around, I didn't want her around for this part. Our little teamwork at the park was great, up until the part where I had to kick Serbian ass. Tempe could have been seriously hurt if things went south. I didn't want that. So I felt a lot better with her on the sidelines.

The train stopped at Cermak, and three hipsters in blue skullcaps came on. They were too cool to sit, so they stood and held onto the railings and talked about the ups and downs of single life. One hipster enjoyed cooking for one, another hipster kept scaring away all his third dates, and the third hipster kept hyping up Tinder and its ability to help him hang out and have some fun. I didn't grasp it at first, but I soon realized that Tinder was for casual encounters. I pledged my full support right there. If both parties were on the same page, sharing a love for mutual physical activity was both efficient and stress-free. Why beat around the bush and play games with someone of minuscule substance? Why chase? I was convinced the third hipster knew all of life's secrets. If things went completely south with Tempe, I'd get back in the saddle and follow the hipster's lead. Like with the poet girl. Fun, effortless, and drama-free. Time would tell. I wanted to ask the hipster how to

Tinder, but then the train stopped and they got off laughing and sprinting up the ramp to their destination. They almost knocked over a short girl in a Hello Kitty backpack.

Two minutes later the train stopped at Clybourn Avenue. I waited for a woman lugging a double stroller, then got off and followed the crowd. I knew the general direction I was going, but I didn't know the landmarks. I was more of a visual navigator—that coffee shop; that bakery; that gas station. That gas station. If I could see the spot, I could find what I was looking for. No spot, no dice. But I took note of the landmarks as I walked.

My destination was in the 1800 block of Clybourn. I checked a street sign and ran the numbers in my head. I might've been the Professor, but my math sucked. It still amazes me that I passed algebra. But if you don't succeed, try, try, again. I was three blocks away.

The more I walked, the happier I got. I walked at a smooth cadence, not too fast, not too slow. Not one person noticed me. Like I was transplanted into an alternate universe where technology didn't exist. I was grateful. I walked past a young couple arguing in Spanish and past a loose pit bull running around trying to lick people and past a gas station with a sign that said "Hep Wanted."

A block later I found it. At first I thought it was all a big joke courtesy of the lockup keeper. He had nothing better to do than fuck around and make people chase paper. But when I looked at the address again, he was right. And I was wrong. The spot I was looking at made for the perfect cover.

It wasn't exactly a warehouse, or even a two flat. It looked like a portable mobile home. I didn't see any wheels on it, but then again with all the technology I missed on the inside, if there was a will there was a way. The maybe-mobile post stood in an enclosed fence area with barbed wire on all sides, and ran parallel to a huge warehouse. But the address on file wasn't the warehouse, it was the command post. The supplemental report said one of the cronies worked there, or his parents did. They kept his inhaler. Which wasn't a bad thing at all, but I wondered what relevance the crony had to Vegas's drug case. They weren't charged, unless the state wanted to make them all co-defendants at some point. Tempe hadn't mentioned anything, and neither had Stine.

I did a stakeout. I had never done one before, but if TV procedurals counted, I was the top name in the game. Find a covert spot and watch. And learn. And figure things out. Simple. No dummies guide needed. I put the file away and found a bench covered by a bush that was last cut when soap shoes were in vogue. I sat there and watched the people milling about. A Rhodesian Ridgeback ran around the premises and licked some of the workers in hard hats leaving the warehouse. The workers petted the dog and made sure to lock the fence on the way out. They didn't check in with the mobile post. Maybe they had time clocks or punch-in stations inside. A man in a dress shirt and construction boots walked around taking notes on a clipboard. Then a young Hispanic kid in yellow shorts bro-hugged one of the hard hat workers before going inside.

Then a white Lexus SUV pulled up, the door to the mobile post opened, and a man in a beanie came out. He had sunglasses on and walked with a slight limp, dragging his left foot. From my vantage I couldn't make a better ID.

But I recognized the man who got out of the Lexus. I'd have known those orange spectacles anywhere, even without a judicial robe.

Judge Romero stepped out of the SUV and shook hands with the man in the beanie. They chatted for a minute like old friends reuniting after getting lost during a tropical storm. Then the beanie man handed Romero an envelope, and the judge went back to his car. He floored it till the dust bunnies said hello for miles, and he was gone.

I was fucked.

Romero wasn't picking up puppies and cupcakes. He was getting double the Benjamins to take me down. Two hundred grand a year to talk shit to lawyers and defendants wasn't enough for him. He must've gotten mixed up in some other racket. My mind ran through a million possibilities, but kept returning to the one that involved me getting the short end of the stick for eternity. Romero might have laid off me initially, but now I fully expected the force of the crooked robe to come crashing down on all my fine features.

Before I could decide what to do next, I felt a gun at the back of my head.

A voice said, "Move, and a concussion will be the least of your worries, boxer man."

33

My hands were tied behind my back, and I was kicked in the knees till they buckled. I was punched in the stomach three times and then blindfolded. Just another day in the life of an amateur sleuth.

The voice said, "You've been fucking with us too long."

I said, "Thanks for the props."

I was punched two more times. A lifetime in the ring taught me to clench my core to cushion the impact. The punches weren't fatal, but they still hurt like a bitch.

I heard more voices and footsteps in the distance. I couldn't make out exactly what they were saying, but it didn't take a genius to put it all together. The cavalry was coming.

Twenty seconds later I was right.

I counted seven different voices. Six were male, but the seventh was an absolute wild card. I wanted to be sensitive to the terminology people used nowadays, so I went with possibly transgendered vocal cords. The voices complained about being summoned for such a shitty job. I smiled because that meant that the voices were inexperienced. Inexperience led to letting your guard down. Letting your guard down led to foolish mistakes. And foolish mistakes led to getting your ass kicked and wishing you were smarter than you actually were.

And all that animus led back to me. Waiting. Smiling. Ready to throw down. When the moment presented itself I'd make my move. Maybe it would take five minutes, maybe it would take fifty-five, but I'd start with the weakest link and work my way outward, like I did at the park.

I was yanked onto my feet. "Walk or your brain will be eating bullets for lunch," the voice said.

"What cadence would you like?" I asked.

I was knocked in the back of the head, and I started walking. Gravel crunched under my feet and stuck to the bottom of my Chelseas. I'd need a fresh set of kicks when this was all said and done. I'd walked about fifty paces before I heard metal clanging and a fence pulling apart. I was in the main compound. Hands pushed me from behind, and I picked up speed. Since the leader didn't have a preferred cadence, I went with a six.

The voices around me got louder. One guy complained about child support, another complained about the Bears not making quarterback a top priority in the draft, and a third guy wished he was in Boca Raton with his cousins. I was tempted to bring up Sid Luckman for a second to keep it old-school. Nah.

Thirty paces later I heard a door open. I was pushed again, and as I continued forward I heard the unmistakable sound of machinery and commerce. I was kicked at the knees again, and I found cement. The door behind me shut with rusty, squeak-filled fanfare.

Then the blindfold came off.

I was surrounded by a bunch of dudes with guns pointed at me. This threw a wrench in my plan to school all their candy asses. The angles weren't right and the timing was completely off. Still, I was the Professor. I might not be able to outrun gun-toting thugs, but I could sure as hell outsmart them. Better to live and learn than to play hero. I'd wait for my opening. I was in no rush to meet my demise.

A man stepped forward. He wore a black beanie cap, sunglasses, and chinos. When he spoke, I recognized his voice as the main one. The leader.

"What I don't appreciate is missing my afternoon smoothie to come all the way out here and deal with bullshit," he said. "A clueless boxer sticking his nose where it doesn't belong."

I tried to get up, but the guns moved closer. Point taken.

I said, "When a man is getting a lap dance and thoroughly enjoying himself, and then he gets a chance to speak to the talent outside the arena, don't fuck it up."

The leader grinned. "You're a wiseass. I like that. But a wiseass can't avoid his fate."

His cronies snickered, and I identified the weak link. One guy stood a little bit farther back than the rest. Some would say that was a matter of semantics or a miscellaneous detail that didn't matter in the grand scheme of things. I begged to differ. This guy wasn't in tune with the rest of the group. Which meant he was an outsider. And outsiders fucked things up. Royally. They couldn't help it. They weren't part of the culture and were prone to mistakes. A bad draw. A botched order. When the floodgates opened, the outsider was the first to cave and turn traitor.

I said, "I've always wanted to do standup at Second City, but I've been a little occupied the last twelve years."

"You're going back, and there's nothing you can do about it," the leader said.

"I'd prefer not to. They don't offer acting classes on the inside. Unless you have connects."

The leader's patience was wearing thin, and that was all

part of my plan. He would put on a show of force next. Maybe a harder punch or a scratch with a switchblade to draw some blood.

Bring it.

Then I'd pounce like a lion and anything goes.

The leader took a few steps closer. "When the boss said you were meddling with the brotherhood, I didn't believe him. What dumbass sticks his nose where it doesn't belong, repeatedly comes up empty, and then keeps coming back for more? Then I realized who we were talking about. A has-been boxer with three brain cells left. Too fucking stupid to know what's good for you. No wonder you fired your lawyer. Right before the biggest trial of your life."

"She has nothing to do with any of this," I said.

The leader smiled. "A man can't control his dick or his mind when he's around a beautiful woman. Goes back to the beginning of time. Your lawyer was good, but it was you or her, and you made your choice. She has *everything* to do with this."

"My lawyer's Gertrude Stevenson," I said. "And when I find her I'm gonna remember the stupid cap you're wearing and I'm gonna make you eat it."

"Good luck with that. You'll be searching quite a while."

"And when I'm done with you, I'm coming for Vegas too."

The leader laughed. "Keep dreaming, boxer man. Vegas is untouchable."

I spit at his feet. "And what does that make you?"

"Undefeated."

Then came the show of force.

The leader lunged at me, but outsiders were outsiders for a reason. They were too dumb and couldn't be trusted. I knew it. And sure enough, when the leader lunged, the outsider thought it was on. He charged with his gun drawn, and I had a split second to react to it all.

I needed less than that.

I sidestepped the outsider and elbowed the leader into next week.

The outsider came back around, and I delivered a crisp left hook to his right jaw that made him drop his gun and go to sleep. I picked up the gun, and used it the only way I knew how. I pistol-whipped the next guy, who came charging from my left, and for good measure dealt a devasting blow to the guy next to him.

The next two guys, to their credit, dropped their guns and raised their fists. Rules were rules, so I tossed my gun aside and threw down. Slip. Jab. Left hook. Right uppercut. The first guy blocked everything, then his luck ran out. I feigned a jab and got him clean with a right. His buddy got me in the back for a second, but I turned around and did a roundhouse punch that sent him staggering back. I liked this guy, though—he was the future leader of the group. He had both the size and the tactical awareness.

He got two clean jabs in, and blood ran down my lower lip. I loved it; it brought me back to Madison Square Garden. No blood, no true fight. Ever. I gave him two uppercuts and a right hook, and he was counting sheep like the loser at the park.

That left two guys, who'd been politely waiting their turn, guns in hand. The first guy fired at me and missed so badly he hit one of his unconscious cronies in the ass. Before he could right the ship, I charged him and tackled him into some freight barrels. I threw five hard body shots, and when he fell to the floor, I went MMA-style. Ground and pound.

And that's where I fucked up. I wasn't in the UFC. Ground and pound didn't protect me on the streets like boxing did. I couldn't keep everybody in my sights. On my fourth ground and pound, I felt the steel blade. It felt ice-cold as it sliced into my back.

The seventh guy said, "I shouldn't have stopped with one reporter."

I turned around to fight the bastard. He must have been behind me when I was first surrounded, because this was the first time I was seeing his face.

It was Carton.

He spit in my face and plunged the knife into my stomach three times.

Everything went black.

34

I woke to tubes in my arms, bright lights, and a cacophony of beeps. A nurse in scrubs stood to my left side, examining a screen. If I didn't know any better I'd say she was related to the poet girl.

She saw my eyes open. "You've had some day, Mr. Gedrin."

I tried to smile. "Adventure is my middle name."

The nurse shook her head. "Adventure almost put you in a box at the county morgue. Those stab wounds were an inch closer to the internal organs, you're a goner."

"How long have I been out?"

"Three hours."

"How?"

The nurse scribbled something onto a clipboard, checked her watch, then scribbled some more. "You can thank your lucky stars a good Samaritan called 911. You caused quite the ruckus, apparently."

"I had them," I said.

"Not quite."

I looked around. I was in a hospital room with a blue

curtain blocking the doorway. Then it morphed into two blue curtains. Maybe three. I couldn't tell.

The nurse followed my gaze. "It's for privacy, champ. We've had a lot of followers come by when they heard the news. Security has been working overtime."

"I'm glad to be of service."

The nurse turned off the screen and pushed it away. The damned thing had wheels and it folded up into a corner with a bunch of wires sticking out.

"Dr. Sanders will stop by in an hour to update you on things. You should be discharged soon. In the meantime, try and relax. You also have a special visitor who's been waiting a while. I can send them away or have them come in. Your call."

I sat up a little straighter in my bed, and my stomach felt like a thousand needles said hello and goodbye at the same time. I winced.

The nurse pointed under the bed rail. "This button's your best friend." She pressed it, and the back of the bed rose up. The needles returned, but less so.

"Thanks. Send my admirer in."

The nurse left, and I grinned like a Cheshire cat. I knew Tempe couldn't escape for long. It had only been a matter of time before she realized that I had good intentions in firing her in front of all the sharks. I did her a favor by going at it solo. But she'd held out longer than I'd expected. Eight plus hours without a single call or text. Now she would bring flowers and I'd talk about Romero and she'd give me some off-the-record advice on what to do. I'd listen and nod my head at all the right moments, but deep down I didn't care about the specifics. I just wanted to see her smile again and to feel her body against mine. I'd power through all the pain if it meant I could have her in my arms.

The curtain pulled back.

It wasn't Tempe.

It was a man with close-cropped hair, a Taylor Swift t-shirt, jeans, a Rolex watch, and Timberland boots. He had insanely pearly whites and he looked like a million bucks. Matter of fact, he was worth a million bucks. Probably a lot more now.

"You fucking asshole," I said.

Mark Sims, my former manager and agent, pulled a bouquet of flowers from behind his back and forced a smile. "You're the toughest sonofabitch I've ever met." He put the flowers on a side table.

We looked at each other in silence. There was so much I wanted to say to Sims, but the stabbing pain in my stomach made it difficult to give a long soliloquy. I imagine there was so much he wanted to say to me too. But nobody made the first move. Twelve years was a damned long time to go without speaking to somebody. Or to visit somebody.

I decided to start there.

"Where the fuck have you been?" I said.

"I'm sorry, Lance."

"Fuck you."

"I didn't know what to do. Sponsors wouldn't touch you with a ten-foot pole. I didn't want to create the appearance—"

"That you gave a shit? Like a normal human being? Your cash cow gets fucked over, and you sit on the sidelines. Now that I'm out, you wanna dip your hand back in."

I first met Sims when I was only sixteen years old. Sal introduced us during a Golden Gloves tournament. I tore up the competition, and it wasn't long before I turned pro. I wanted to fight, but Sims wanted me to do a peanuts commercial, and a Tide commercial, and a McDonald's commercial. He was the best at getting the suits to put up or shut up. He saw the potential in me, and he was an expert at communicating to the highest bidder. He took a chance on an unproven kid, and he'd made bank ever since. Sims worked hard and deserved all the accolades.

But he also high-tailed it back to L.A. the minute I was arrested.

"People make mistakes," he said. "I fucked up. I own that."

"Damned right," I said.

As much as I wanted to mess with him some more, I knew that Sims held the keys to the one thing I'd truly wanted from the moment I got back out. Sure, there was Stevenson and Stine and Vegas and my liberty to deal with. But before all that shit happened, I'd had only one purpose.

My title. That I never lost. I wanted it back.

The road to redemption would be long and hard, but it would be worth it. I could still fight.

Sims sat down and looked out the window. The sun was still out and there wasn't a cloud in the sky. "You sure gave them hell," he said.

"Fucker got me from behind," I said. "Stevenson's ex."

"Nope. Her ex moved back to Green Bay a year ago. His family's got a farm up there."

I took Sims's word for it. He had the connects. The trail wasn't that warm after all.

"You never had good eyes in the back of your head," Sims continued. "Remember Lopez?"

Of course I remembered Lopez. It was my first pro fight, in a small strip mall in the middle of Shitsville. I kicked ass, and then a couple Mexican cousins of the guy I'd just dispatched bum-rushed the ring before security woke up from their siesta. Cousin Lopez thought it would be fun to bring a pair of brass knuckles into the fray. I dropped him so hard that the knuckles fell into his mouth and he looked like a suckling pig. The other cousin ran away and never looked back. I kept the brass knuckles as a souvenir.

"Viva Mexico," I said.

We shared a laugh.

Then Sims said, "I'm back, Lance. For real this time. Trust me."

"I'm not signing shit."

Sims nodded. "I get that. We'll deal with the specifics later. First things first, stop acting stupid and get yourself a fucking lawyer."

And just like that Sims *was* back. Barking orders and trying to steer me into good decisions. I'd missed that. Being an only child was rough sometimes. But Sims was like my sibling by proxy.

"I know my case inside and out," I said.

"You don't know the technicalities."

"I know *corpus delicti*."

"That shit won't save you this time. Carpetopoulos has had years to work up this case."

"He can work it up till he has gray whiskers. Zero still equals zero, last time I checked."

"I've made a short list of the top criminal lawyers in the city. They've been calling me offering to represent you pro bono. I gave them your consent to review all the discovery on such short notice. They're salivating over the details."

"I don't have the discovery," I said.

Sims shook his head. "When you were singing in your sleep with all that shit the doc has you on, your old firm came by here with seven boxes of discovery. They had to tender it back over since you're *pro se*. For now. I brought in my assistants on over-time, and they copied all the discovery and shipped it off to the hungry lawyers. They don't want the case, then they destroy the discovery. Easy."

My heart fluttered. "Who delivered the boxes?"

Sims shrugged. "Some clueless secretary who got the short

end of the stick. No partners and associates wanted to do the honors. I wouldn't either, under the circumstances." He'd been a lawyer before he decided to agent and manage.

"That's cool," I said.

We sat there for a few minutes shooting the shit and reminiscing about the good ole days. We cracked jokes and talked about the future. We were both on the same page. Then I went back to the very beginning and ran through everything. Step by step. From the moment I got out. I left no stone unturned. I told him about the pancakes and potato science experiments and "Carton" and Stevenson and the tattoo kid and Romero. Sims nodded through it all, and when I was done he stood.

"When you're discharged, you're staying with me till the case is over. We have a lot of work to do."

"My stay may be short-lived," I said.

He shook his head. "No. I let you go down for something you didn't do the first time. No chance in hell I'm gonna let that happen again. You're gonna have an army of lawyers if that's what it takes. They wanna come for you, they better fucking bring their A game."

I smiled. "Stock the fridge with OJ."

35

Four hours later I was officially discharged. There were a bunch of words on a bunch of papers, but I had no intention of reading them. I had a migraine from all the drugs and my stomach felt like concrete. My cheering section outside the hospital included a high school football team, two Navy veterans, a retired police officer, a nun, a cook, and Sandy from the Pink Purse. I didn't count the sharks. A buff nurse pushed me out in a wheelchair and I gave my best smile. A thumbs-up, too. Sandy kissed me on the cheek and gave me some flowers. "Hang in there" was uttered so many times from so many different people that for a minute I thought it was my middle name.

An Escalade pulled up, and the nurse opened the back door. I ditched the wheelchair and got in. The sharks got hungrier with their flashes and questions, and who could blame them. I'd gone from champ to prison to shopping at the clearance rack to retried for murder to surviving a vicious attack from a bunch of thugs. Maybe I'd write a novel about it someday.

Twenty-four minutes later I was at Sims's place. The Escalade went south into an alley and then found a garage on the left-hand side. It picked up speed for a moment, then stopped all the way in the back corner of the garage. My door swung open.

"Right this way, Mr. Gedrin," the chauffeur said.

I followed obediently. Sims was all show. He could never do simple things like a mere mortal, so everything had its own twist to it. Picking me up became grand ceremony. Then and now. The chauffeur led me through three doors to a private elevator. We hopped in and took it all the way to the top. The doors opened to a luxury high-rise penthouse overlooking the lake. The place was smack dab in the center of the Gold Coast. Sims loved excess and I loved critiquing it.

"Take care, Mr. Gedrin," the chauffeur said as he departed.

Sims said, "You look like shit."

"Gracias."

He led me to a kitchen fit for multiple kings. "Eat whatever you want. I'm getting the files." He disappeared up a flight of winding stairs that led to outer space. Life was sweet when you repped the champ.

I opened the fridge and found items from all over the food pyramid. Apples. Oranges. Pastas. Grains. Beans. Legumes. Meats. Fish. Yogurts. Guac. Everything had an organic label on it, and everything was magazine-worthy. Emeril would be proud. Sal wasn't in my head this time so I went with pasta and chicken thighs. I went to town on it, and four minutes later my stomach regretted my zeal.

Sims came down the stairs with a banker's box.

"I thought there were seven," I said.

"Fuck off," he said. "These are the mental impressions of all the attorneys that have reviewed the case. Their notes and commentary. Summaries. They work fast. We pick one, and they'll file an appearance with the clerk first thing tomorrow morning."

"They must be starving," I said.

"Mr. Green can be pretty convincing."

"I'll bet."

"I told all the attorneys who consulted to give me their theory of the case and to describe their trial strategy in a nutshell. It's all in the box."

Sims pulled a tall stack of files from the box and plopped them on the counter. There were millions of color-coded Post-its all over the various pages. I took a file from the bottom, but Sims stopped me. "From the top. Everybody gets their fair shake."

"How about the middle?" I said.

"No. Submission one, page one. These lawyers are all different, but they all have something that can help. Keep your mind open. They prepped all this in an hour, man."

I knew Sims was right. As much as I doubted complete strangers coming onto my case, I knew that all my lawyers were the same once upon a time: complete strangers who took the time to gain my trust and rapport. I started at the top.

The first lawyer candidate who wanted to save me from life without parole was a Peoria native. Fifteen years in a thriving solo practice. Hard worker. His bio was boring and had seven spelling errors in it. If I were to play Russian roulette with a bunch of suits, I at least wanted one with connections to Chicago. Maybe one who even knew Carpetopoulos and could slap him in the side of the head and get him to come to his senses and toss the bullshit case.

"No dice," I said.

"He beat a case before the US Supreme Court," Sims said.

"They don't care about that in Crook County."

I picked up another packet. A lawyer based in the Monadnock building. Right across from the Dirksen Courthouse. Big-time drug defense lawyer. Twenty years' experience. Which would have made him a decent candidate, but then I saw his photo. I didn't like his ratchet smile, so I tossed it aside.

"Already?" Sims said.

"A jury sees that fake smile, I'm done. Shysters are shysters."

Sims agreed with me on that one and handed me another file. The next one looked much more promising. A grizzled veteran with forty years of experience, more than twenty of them on murders alone. He'd written *corpus delicti* on the file in three spots, and I smiled. Then the lawyer scribbled something about faulty science and error rates in testing certain samples. He was the real deal.

"Wesley Andrews," Sims said. "Voted one of the top criminal lawyers in Illinois by his peers and various bar associations. Problem is he's out of town and is going to need a big-ass retainer up front to fly in from Aruba."

Of course.

I said, "Fuck him. I can do this myself. I know all the testimony."

Sitting in court for weeks on end while your life is being decided is no small task. I used the time to remember every facial feature and tic of every witness who took the stand. I could recite their testimony from scratch, and knew that I'd never forget a word of it as long as I kept kicking.

Sims shook his head and gave me another file. And another. And another. It went like that for another twenty minutes. When we were finished with all the candidates, we were in a far worse place than when we'd started. Our theory of the case was more confusing, and at one point I even found myself giving props to Carpetopoulos. I brought Romero up to Sims a couple times, and he kept saying that we couldn't bank on that.

The judge would be switched and the case would go on. Lawyers had all sorts of tricks. Without a smoking gun, I'd go on trial no matter what.

We took a break, and Sims showed me his state-of-the-art high-def TV. It literally took up a whole wall in his lavish quarters. Who needed the motel keeper package with twelve channels? No bueno. Sims turned it on and we watched the Lakers game. They were in the West finals and were kicking ass. Staples Center was poppin' and the Laker girls were showing off all sorts of new moves. Sims offered me a beer, but I declined. Pills and alcohol never mixed. I grabbed some OJ from the fridge and got some much-needed vitamin C.

We watched for another five minutes, but then we both got bored when it became a complete blowout.

Sims pulled a disc from a drawer. "How about a classic?" he said.

"I thought you'd never ask."

He placed the disc into a contraption to the right of the TV. The disc made a scraping noise for a second, then whirred like an airplane. When the image crystallized on screen, I knew Sims made the right call.

My first title fight.

The MGM Grand.

Goluka v. Gedrin.

I was twenty pounds lighter back then, but my right hand was ten times stronger. The bell rang and Michael Buffer announced us to the world. Goluka got twice the cheers. He'd had the belt for three years straight at that point.

We got down to business.

Goluka was a tall brutish Polack who didn't know when to quit.

I had crab fisherman in my blood.

We exchanged hundreds of punches in the first four

rounds. They didn't have Compubox back in those days, so I did the calculations in my head. Goluka was ahead one hundred punches landed to ninety-seven. The cards were pretty even, but I needed a hellacious finish to win over the judges. Sal slapped me in the corner and told me to wake the fuck up. I was a demon in the fifth. I connected with a flurry of left hooks, jabs, and rights. Normally my opponents would tire out and leave themselves open to going to sleep. But Goluka was experienced, and the fight drew on.

"This is the best part," Sims said.

I agreed.

Goluka tried bear-hugging me late in the fifth. I slipped him and connected with such a big uppercut that he fell onto the ropes. The crowd went wild. But Goluka wasn't done. He shook it off and got me with a couple jabs. He backed me into the corner, and I could hear Sal swearing in every Mediterranean language known to man. Goluka got me with a body shot, but then I got him in the right kidney with a body shot of my own. I slipped him and threw as many combinations as I could. The crowd ate it up. I threw one more hard right, and Goluka's corner threw in the towel because the Polack didn't know how to protect himself for his own good.

TKO.

My corner put me on their shoulders, and I got the belt twelve seconds later.

Then the coverage went to replay. This part I'd never seen before. At the time I was just so damned happy I got the win. The camera panned to shots of the crowd eating up the seconds before the knockout. It paused on a high roller in a suit. Which wasn't surprising in any way. Rich people liked boxing. It made them think they had more balls than they really had. Maybe the guy was part owner of the hotel.

But I barely noticed the high roller; my attention was

drawn to the woman next to him. Somebody I never would have expected. Life is fucking filled with surprises. Some shock you to the core.

As Goluka was getting his brains bashed in, the man in the suit shook his head. He probably lost a lot of money that night.

And then he turned and kissed his woman.

Gertrude Stevenson.

36

She had long brunette locks and her eyes didn't have dark circles under them back then, but when she smiled after locking lips with the high roller, I knew it was her. Drugs or no drugs, I'd never forget those pearly whites.

"Sure took you long enough," Sims said.

"How many more skeletons do you have in your closet?" I said.

Sims went silent for a moment, then paused my classic fight. "I didn't think it mattered at the time. And I didn't want to mess with your head later, when things went south."

"My lawyer knew me before I knew her. How is that not a big deal?"

"She was a groupie. I guess the proper term is sugar baby now. She'd hang around all the high rollers at the top clubs in Vegas. Spend time with them. Make their wildest dreams come true. She so happened to become a kickass lawyer. But back then she was in law school trying to make ends meet.

I didn't know what was worse: the growing pain in my

stomach or the fact that Sims knew all this back then and kept it quiet till now.

"Who's that loser she's with? He's showing too much chest hair, and that slicked-back look is stupid."

"Eduardo Zarta. A rich playboy from New Jersey. One of the most powerful men in the business world. But not for the reasons you'd think."

Sims walked to the kitchen and returned with some grapes. He offered me some and I shook him off.

"Zarta is Irish mob, but he runs his racket only with Serbians and nobody tells him shit. His mom got snatched by a cartel in the eighties, and a group of Serbian footballers happened upon her and fought off all the captors. They returned her safe and sound, and Zarta's been partial to the Serbs ever since. Rumor has it he runs drugs all up the East Coast and into Canada. On paper, he's in pharmaceuticals. You don't wanna double-cross him. A lot of people are in his debt. Hence the ringside seats to the hottest ticket in town."

I needed a smoking gun, and dammit I had it.

"And he paid off the cops to look the other way when he murdered Stevenson?" I asked.

"Not quite."

"Whose side are you on here?"

"I don't play sides, Lance. I play common sense. The legal side of me can't resist. You know that. Zarta had a rock-solid alibi the minute Stevenson went missing."

"He was out killing others so some other dude killed her. The SODDI defense. Solid."

"No. Zarta was in Greece for two months peddling some state-of-the-art libido pill to expand his empire. Better than Viagra and would keep you harder than Valyrian steel. His flight records match up. The Greek police were briefed and they ran surveillance on him while he was out there. Nobody bought the shit he was selling. So he hit the beach every day and had a different Greek woman in his villa every night."

"And Carpetopoulos was there eating souvlaki and saganaki by his side." Sims was full of shit sometimes, but his recon was so thorough that I couldn't poke any holes in it. Damned lawyers and their analytical brains.

Sims continued. "Also, Stevenson's body still hasn't been recovered, so the cops are technically still treating it as a missing persons case, despite the adage that if somebody isn't found within the first forty-eight hours, it becomes a homicide investigation. CPD has nothing else to go on. She repped a lot of shitty people, but she got such good results, the odds of any one of them just offing her isn't consistent. Plus, a lot of lawyers hit the bottle hard and never come back from it. Depression. Anxiety. She had so many demons. Don't forget that."

I got up from the couch, and the needles hit my stomach again.

"When do you take your next round of pills?" Sims asked.

"Whenever my heart desires. You my mama now too?"

Sims smiled, and I flicked him off. I went to the kitchen counter and grabbed my pill bottle. I popped two pills and gulped some water down. I found saltine crackers next to the bottle and added them as insurance for the needles. The bottle said take once every three hours. I didn't want to wake up in the middle of the night messing with my REM cycle so I figured two should cover it.

"He can only get lucky for so long," I said. "Zarta's hands are clean on paper, but his cronies are bound to slip up. Lawyering 101."

"True."

I walked back to the couch and lay down.

"Take the guest bedroom," Sims said.

"I don't like big spaces." While Sims had been partying

with the world's elite all these years, my party was in a six-by-eight steel hellhole. As far as I was concerned, smaller spaces were much more fitting. And Sims's couch was still a huge step up from the motels I'd called home for the last week.

"I'll call Wesley and tell him to get his ass in from Aruba. Weather is shit there anyway this time of year."

"Yeah, yeah."

Sims smiled and pulled out his phone. He typed faster than Tempe, Stine, and the poet girl combined. When he finished, he walked to a closet next to the kitchen and pulled out a few pairs of boxing gloves and threw them to me. My coordination was so off from the drugs, they hit me in the face.

"Sign 'em, champ. They're going for twenty g's a pop with everything that's happening."

"What's my cut?"

"One hundred percent. For now. We have to strike while the iron's hot."

Money was money, and I never was allergic to it. I signed all the gloves and tossed them back to Sims. He put them in boxes and left them by his front door.

"My assistants will be here in five minutes to get them out of here."

"Cool."

Sims looked at his screen again. After a minute he turned back to me. "And you need a fucking phone."

"I have one."

"A reliable one."

"The kid at the store said it's the best flip phone in its class."

Sims shook his head. "Do you want iOS or Android?"

I looked at him like he had a communicable disease.

"Apple or no?" he asked.

I said, "I want orange."

Sims dropped the subject and told me he was doing the nightly news. Controlling the narrative. The sharks knew he was repping me again, and they were salivating for more.

"Where are the rest of your classics?" I said.

Sims pointed to the drawer where he got the first disc. "I've got them all there. From no crowd to the end. You're one hell of an entertainer."

I laughed, and Sims took off.

Three minutes later two young assistants in matching glasses came to pick up the boxes. They weren't heavy, and there was no need for two people to do it, but Sims did everything his way or the highway. Since he was paying, I didn't debate the need for two assistants with the actual assistants.

When they were gone, I took my phone out and tried to find anything I could on Zarta. He was a ghost in an age when everybody was online. After two hours of futility, I went back to the classics.

I popped in the disc from my second pro fight. Right after the Lopez fiasco. Laughter was the best medicine sometimes. Madison Square Garden. But even for the Garden, the undercard didn't bring a lot of people out. That, or there was still a line at the door to get into the place.

Johnson v. Gedrin.

Johnson was a long, thin black kid with rock-hard abs and a silver jaw. He talked a lot of shit and promoters saw nothing but dollar signs in his future—and theirs.

I was still inexperienced in those days, from a technical standpoint.

But Johnson was more so.

The fight lasted two minutes and twenty-eight seconds. I improved to two and oh in my career, and I knocked the shit out of Johnson so bad that the medics had to cart him out of the ring. The promoters wanted every piece of me after that, but I wanted absolutely zero piece of them.

The camera panned to the crowd. The few in attendance cheered and pumped their fists. This time I was looking for her. For Stevenson. Along with some high roller.

She wasn't there. But Zarta was. A little thinner, but with the same hair grease and chest hair sticking out. The asshole was messing with me. And when he turned to kiss his woman, I knew right then and there that I'd cross paths with Zarta sooner or later. I'd ask all the questions and he'd give all the answers.

Zarta didn't kiss Stevenson that night.

He kissed Amy Pako.

Before I could make sense of it, the drugs kicked in and I closed my eyes.

37

The next morning my stomach felt less like concrete and more like runaway sand finding its sweet spot. The meds were working wonders. I rubbed the crust out of my eyes, stretched my back, neck, quads, hammies, and groin, and then devoured a Denver omelet that was on Sims's counter. He knew that the quickest way to get in my good graces was with his patented breakfast of champions, and his battle with the sharks last night hadn't messed with his cooking skills one bit. Bravo. I'd thank him when he got back from the office. Sims was already at work, no doubt barking orders and taking names. He lived by the adage that people should sleep when they're dead. I lived by the adage that sleep was spectacular.

After eating, I changed clothes and went to Connors Park. The small, triangular piece of land was a block away from Sims's place. At first glance, it had nothing on Jonquil. No playground for the kids. No basketball court. No soccer field. No baseball field. No sunbathers. But there was a fountain. And benches. And the place was from the 1800s, which made for excellent scenery. I walked slowly to take it all in.

The events of last night didn't fully register until the omelet had fully registered. I didn't believe in coincidences, and the tapes had proven me right. Zarta, without a shadow of a doubt, killed Amy Pako. And Stevenson, too. His fake alibi meant nothing; he'd simply ordered his cronies to do his dirty work while he was abroad. The mobster had risen up the ranks with his cunning and deceit. He'd conned a lot of people. But he wasn't conning me. I wanted to go back to the warehouse and politely say my piece to all his loser minions. I'd start with the Carton wannabe, and I'd go through everything, step by step, until all cards were on the table. And then the ball would be back in Zarta's court. The connection to Amy Pako and Stevenson was unmistakable. I had a feeling it was with Stine, too.

One man, three women.

Two in a box. The other in the wind.

Zarta had dirty hands, and dirty hands meant supreme arrogance. And supreme arrogance meant supreme fuckups. And it wasn't just limited to outsiders. Zarta had framed me for Amy Pako's murder, and he'd ordered hits on Stevenson and Stine. On paper it sounded so simple. But my job was to figure it all out and put his ass behind bars. Circumstantial evidence wasn't enough. I needed the smoking gun, or else I'd never get to the Space Needle.

I saw a school of squirrels attacking the biggest walnuts I'd ever seen. The walnuts must have been juiced up somewhere in the production process, and the squirrels didn't mind. As I continued walking I saw a couple breaking up, another couple holding hands, and then what looked like a possible couple-to-be walking awkwardly on a first date. The universe was telling me something.

I took my phone out and texted Tempe. It had been a full twenty-four hours now with no contact. She was probably just walking into the office.

Sup, cutie, I texted.

She didn't text back.

Yet.

When I reached the end of the park, my stomach felt so good I decided to push it. I went back to the park entrance and started again. I did the math and figured that eight revolutions was a decent workout and would test my recovery.

I was forty-five feet in when my phone rang. My body tingled for a minute, then stopped.

No dice with Tempe.

Dice with an unknown number.

I was an equal-opportunity communicator, so I picked up. "Hello?"

"Mr. Gedrin? It's Wesley Andrews. I'm back from Aruba and on the way to the clerk's office now. Mark brought me up to speed, but I need to speak to you pronto to go over all the details before the trial. Answering ready like this is the craziest fucking thing I've ever seen, but we'll do it."

I'd completely forgotten about the shysters we'd been researching last night. Mark had picked Andrews, and I'd said yes. The drugs did too.

"Pick a time and a place and I'm there," I said.

"Meet me at my office in an hour. Monadnock building. You know where that is, right? Right across from Dirksen. This case is weak shit. We're gonna kick ass left and right."

"*Corpus delicti*," I said.

Andrews laughed and hung up. He'd be checking his watch in an hour and I'd be checking the latest fashion trends online. I was becoming quite adept at searching things on my flip phone. Andrews would have to make do without me. With forty years' experience, he'd be all right. And if not, I'd bitch at Sims and Sims would bitch at him. Ah, the beauty of celebrity.

I kept walking, and a minute later I stopped at a bench and did some pushups. Absolute fail. Instead of hammering out something in the triple digits like normal, I barely got half that. No bueno. The girl who'd had her heart broken passed me. I asked her where she got the pretzel in her hand, and she gave it to me, crying. She called me names that were reserved for the breaker-upper, and I thanked her for the pretzel. Then she ran off.

So much for my charm.

My stomach didn't need the pretzel, but the small bites I took seemed to help. The sodium counterbalanced the grease from Sims's omelet. Sims was a health nut, or had been once, but now he was slacking.

Two minutes later I crossed back to the front of the park.

And that's when I saw it.

A black SUV with tints.

Out-of-state plates.

It slowed at the corner opposite the park entrance and stopped, idling. A conscientious driver would have pulled as close to the curb as possible, but not this one. The SUV sat at a weird angle, its flashers on. Cars weaved around it like a serpent. A bus, too. Then a CPD car meandered over and gave a warning shot, and the SUV was gone.

The needles in my stomach came back again. I looked at my phone. Still nothing from Tempe. Maybe she had another dep, or maybe everybody was in the conference room regrouping and trying to come to terms with it all. They probably had a psychologist on staff to maximize productivity and minimize the bullshit distractions.

I realized I had unfinished business.

I grabbed a cab to my former firm.

38

The cab driver wasn't into the Bulls, Blackhawks, Bears, or Cubs. But he was all about the White Sox. Stickers lined the glass partition, and a pair of fuzzy dice hung from his rearview mirror. The radio was tuned to ESPN 1000, but the volume was so low an elephant couldn't hear.

"The minute they went from Comiskey to U.S. Cellular I knew my White Sox were done. Who the hell does that?" the cabbie said.

"Commerce and stupidity are the best bedfellows."

"Then the assholes change the name to Guaranteed Rate Field. They might as well jump off a bridge. All those prick executives. Selling mortgages and tickets and hotdogs all in the same stadium. Unbelievable."

"Bring back Ozzie and Paulie. The roof exploded when he hit that grand slam."

The cab driver smiled and bobbed his head. "Hell yeah. Those were the days. Before Ubers and things."

I smiled too. I was at Pontiac when Paul Konerko hit a

grand slam against the Houston Astros in the World Series. I saw it through the rusty steel bars of my cell and would never forget it. Guards and inmates came together for a few seconds the way rabid dogs and feral cats did when they found a free meal in the open. Pure bliss.

The cab driver picked up speed and weaved around other cabbies with such precision that for a moment I thought we were at the Indy 500. I looked back every quarter block for the Black SUV with no tints. Nada. If the SUV got bold though, I pledged all my support to this White Sox fan to spring me outta trouble. The SUV was fucking with me—or maybe the drugs were. Rebounding off all the toxins and ingredients was no bueno.

Eight minutes later the cab driver pulled up in front of the firm. I tipped him generously, and he was gone. I presented my now-defunct ID to the security honchos in front and told them I needed to pick up some personal belongings. They stared me down for a long beat before letting me up. I didn't need any help decoding their stares and muted whispers. *A murderer is walking through. The fucking scumbag.* Like they didn't see other unsavory characters walk these hallowed halls to see their lawyers every day.

I took the elevator to the fifth floor, where all was quiet. But the secretary was in.

"Mr. Gedrin, pleasure to see you, sir." Her nostrils flared like a rhinoceros's and I could've sworn I saw steam coming out of them too.

"I came to pick up some things." Yeah right.

The secretary typed something into her computer and nodded. "ID has already been deposited downstairs. Now hand over any excess files you have in your possession."

"How do you define possession?"

The secretary gave me a murderous look. "In your possession or control. On or about your person. Clear? My notes say the Vegas file is still outstanding."

"I don't know anything about a Vegas file. I can tell Ms. Tempe all about it."

The secretary looked like she'd seen a ghost. "Ms. Tempe is not with us anymore."

"No. I saw her yesterday."

The secretary nodded. "I understand your frustration, Mr. Gedrin. It's been getting crazier and crazier around here lately. I can't get into details, but she no longer works here, effective late yesterday. She tendered her resignation."

"She didn't give two weeks?"

"I'm just the messenger," the secretary said.

"I really don't have the Vegas file anymore." Ha ha.

"Then our business is done here. If the Vegas file happens to materialize in the future, please destroy it. I shouldn't be the one to tell you confidentiality is confidentiality."

We shook hands, and that's all she wrote. It was a run for the ages. I made the record books for briefest tenure at one of the top law firms in the city. I fought the machine and investigated the hell out of whatever I was assigned. Ultimately I wasn't a good fit and pursued other passions. That's how I'd write it anyway. A bona fide bestseller. The sharks would love it.

I thanked the secretary and asked if I could take one of the paintings on the wall as a souvenir. She said no, and I rode the elevator down alone. It must have been clean-your-office day because on the third floor, five janitors in matching uniforms got on with their carts, squishing me into one of the corners. They spoke in code and stared at me the whole way down.

I didn't say goodbye to the security douchebags.

When I came out of the revolving doors, I ran into

Murdock. He was smoking right next to a poorly planted perennial in front of the building.

"My brotha," he said. "What the fuck happening with that state's attorney?"

"He's been eating too much baklava. Bogus charges. All day, every day. I'll be ready."

Murdock smiled and took another drag of his cigarette. "They say things get easier when you come out, but them habits are hard to break. I still bench press like Ronnie, you feel me? But I get so nervous sometimes I gotta smoke and eat some Mickey D's. My momma don't like it."

"The rib sandwich is top-notch. All natural, not that rubbery shit."

We shared a laugh, and for a minute I wished we were both on the yard putting on a show for the other cons. Being on stage was fun sometimes.

Then Murdock said, "What's up with your girl?"

"Who?"

"Don't give me that. I wasn't born yesterday. I saw the way y'all been looking at each other in that conference room. She wanted to drop them panties right there if she could. If we weren't in that room, she would have."

I shook my head. "My success with the ladies has been the biggest parabola of all time."

Murdock was confused, but then he got it. "Women be crazy, but damn they be so fine though. When I got out, my boys lined me up with women from the neighborhood. Charity work. But man, I want a real woman. With a degree and shit. With principles."

"Yeah."

"Your girl up and quit like that." Murdock snapped his fingers. "Good money and now nothing. A couple partners be talking to me, then she come in with one of those rages. I seen it before. Bitches be crazy sometimes. I saw them eyes. She been bustin' her ass and not appreciated. She threw some paper on the table, signed it. Then ripped it up."

It sounded like classic Tempe, so I didn't doubt it.

"But that's why they brought me here," Murdock continued. He tossed his cigarette into the perennial soil. So much for protecting the environment. "Them partners don't trust her. Missing work. Goofy. Not a team player, brotha. They wanted me to track her. She was my special assignment. About a week before you got here."

I said, "That's impossible. She's the top associate at the firm. Ready to make partner."

Murdock shook his head. "Them partners want another partner, they put 'em in court to develop. Why you think your girl was never in court? She be pushing papers. She no Stevenson, brotha. And she got a record like you wouldn't believe. Fooled the bar and the firm—and me, till I found it. Nothing fool me forever."

My mind wasn't registering what Murdock was saying, and my stomach was rapidly regressing. "You can't fool the bar. They're in charge of all the shysters."

Murdock smiled. "Brotha, she fooled them and then some. Believe that."

"Where did you track her?"

"Before court, after court. In the office them partners be keeping her in check. But boy is she something. Girl be walking out of her condo disheveled, looking like shit, then next morning dressed to the nines. Every day like that. Nasty."

"She was letting her hair down." I knew better than to question a woman's style choices, but Murdock didn't hold back.

"She threatened one of them reporters one time, and they got an order of protection against her. Girl had her own cases, but the firm be sweeping it all under the rug. Still fighting them cases on her behalf now."

I wanted to dismiss all this crazy shit offhand. But Murdock didn't pull punches, and he didn't bullshit for the sake of bullshitting. He was real all day every day. And he wasn't getting paid based on me signing gloves and kicking ass in a squared circle. Tempe was sassy and smart and sexy with an edge. But this kind of edge I didn't see. Maybe I'd been drinking the damned Kool-Aid too much. Stine warned me.

I said, "She never hurt anybody."

Murdock shrugged. "After yesterday, everybody worried. Them partners think she gonna come firing like that asshole in Elgin. Remember? Them partners don't have the best security down here neither."

"What do you know about security?"

"Brotha I have a concealed carry permit now. And my cousin be hired for extra security around the premises in case she comin' back for something. God bless America. Land of opportunity."

"She's not gonna do that."

"Nobody knows anybody these days. Real talk," Murdock said. "Except you, champ. You a fighter, plain and simple."

"Same," I said. "I want to speak to her. Say my piece. I fired her yesterday. That has something to do with it."

"Her problems been brewin' a long time, brotha. A girl don't act like that now she's grown. She been acting like that. But you wanna talk, I have the code."

"What?"

"You think I be tracking her with my mind? She ditched the condo last night and ain't never been back. Them partners gave me some device and I slipped it in that girl's purse first day on the job. I told them partners it was an illegal search. They say I'm no cop so it don't matter."

Ah, the technicalities.

"Where is she?" I asked.

Murdock looked around like he was revealing presidential secrets. Then he said, "She at Stevenson's place. She been there since ten last night. Still in mourning I guess. Hasn't left."

"Want an adventure?" I said.

Murdock shook his head. "I don't do no more drama, brotha. Got my fill on the inside. Now I want them checks and them weekends off."

I nodded and bro-hugged him. He gave me Stevenson's address.

And I was gone.

39

I didn't need a cab or an Uber. Stevenson's place was three blocks from the firm, nestled in the heart of River North. The building was twenty stories high, overlooking the Chicago River, and it made Mark's place look like it had training wheels. I was greeted outside by a pair of Chihuahuas disobeying their owner's every command. I tiptoed around them, avoiding their yappy jaws, and slipped inside the building.

The full security team must have been on vacation or putting out imaginary fires for its affluent residents, because as I walked past only one lone security guard sat in the lobby, and he had one eye closed and the other eye glued to *People* Magazine. I took the elevator to the top floor. The whole way up I was mesmerized by the virtual display of the Windy City across its walls. With each floor came new buildings and landmarks on a timeline. It was virtual construction at its finest. The final image featured the construction of the current building and its finished product. A renaissance place for the stars. If you want the cool factor, you have to be at this place, the blurb on the wall read. *"Celebreyfic."* The name was bogus, but life was filled with mirages for the rich and famous. They craved them the way a baby craves a pacifier or a mouse its cheese.

When the doors opened, I stepped out into a long marble hallway with translucent light on both sides. I felt like I was in Star Wars, heading for the mothership. As I walked I was careful not to touch anything and risk getting electrocuted for violating the rules. Then I hit a snag.

A heavy-duty door with a keypad.

The ticket in always came with a price.

The keypad was standard-issue. No tricks. No games. But annoying. I entered my birthdate and pressed enter. Nada. My mom's DOB. Nada. My dad's. Nada. Mark's. Nada. Murdock's Nada. I would have stood there for an eternity to find the right codes. I knew there were millions of combinations and I would have tried every one. But luck is contagious sometimes. I examined the keypad some more and noticed there wasn't any red lighting anywhere.

The keypad was green.

Green for go.

In security parlance that meant the system was disabled, either in person or from afar. Manually or remotely. The obvious follow-up question was whether it was done with or without authorization. A few seconds later I found my answer. The door was open a crack, and there were some smudges on the knob. Manual, then.

I pushed the door open and peeked inside. I expected Henri to come bolting from a side cave somewhere and knock me down like a rag doll, but everything was quiet. I closed the door behind me, and it locked automatically. A matching keypad on the inside now said the system was enabled. A red light flashed three times, and I felt like I'd entered a fortress.

I walked down a hallway that could've been from the feudal ages when visitors had to walk through long corridors of great ceremony. This led to a room the size of half a basketball court with white leather sectionals and a big-screen TV that rivaled Sims's.

I looked around for Tempe. I called out Henri's name. I checked the balcony for any late-night parties. I checked the first bedroom, then the second bedroom, third, and fourth. Stevenson sure did well for herself.

And then I found the master bedroom—but the door was locked. No bueno. The only people I knew who locked their bedroom door were annoying teenagers and those wanting some quality adult time, but I didn't hear anything of the latter from behind the door.

I kicked the door in just the right spot. It flew right off the hinges. I should've tried out for the Bears.

The master bedroom was half the size of the main hallway and lined with appliances and electronics. Pure excess. The king bed held pristine sheets and a solid duvet.

And Tempe.

She was sitting on the bed pretzel-style, her back to me. Quiet. She was obviously aware of my grand entrance but didn't show it.

"Long time," I said.

Silence.

"Relieving you of your services was a dick move. I know that. But it had to be done. You got me?"

Tempe moved a couple inches on the bed, but her back was still to me. The silent treatment was the absolute worst.

"We cool?" I said.

Still nothing from Tempe. I wanted to pull her into my arms and tell her everything would be okay. That I saw a future together for the two of us. We were a great fit and could go the distance maybe. After I beat my case. I wasn't always a good listener, but with her I'd be golden. Promise. I stood there for a few moments trying to figure out the best way to organize my words. I was like a kid at the spring social with a million butterflies.

Tempe stirred.

Then she turned around.

She was pressing a gun to her head.

40

I didn't have a degree in crisis intervention, and for the first time in my life I wished I'd hit the books instead of the ring. As Tempe stood up with the gun pressed to her temple, I held up my hands like one of those helpless chaps in the movies. Tears streamed down her cheeks, smearing her makeup and creating black blobs of insanity under her eyelashes. Her hair was disheveled and her fragrance was tragic. She was in the same suit she'd worn to court yesterday, but she'd done a number on it.

"Please," I said.

"Shut up."

She grimaced in pain, but she wasn't hurt. She closed her eyes for three seconds, then opened them. I should have taken the opportunity to tackle her and wrestle the gun away, but I was too slow and my heroic moment passed faster than I could say please again.

Tempe pulled the gun away from her temple, then pressed it there again. "My whole life people looked down on me," she said. "Since first grade, all the kids knew I was different. My mom called me special. My dad called me Wonder Woman. But there's no shielding yourself from mean girls and boys. They're ruthless creatures. They play favorites and they tell it like it really is."

She took a half step towards me. I still had my hands up, and my brain was still figuring out what to do. Damn the CTE.

"Some days were better than others. I'd show up, color with the other kids. Play kickball at recess. I was a hell of a batter. But then the sun would go down and I wouldn't be able to get out of bed. My parents would prod me with cookies and chocolate and toys, but I couldn't do it. It was like this dark cloud shone its spotlight on me and threw all its spikes and knives too. I'd manage to get out of my funk hours later, and I'd go in late to class. All eyes on me again. The taunts. The gossip. The laughter. 'You got a late pass again? Why?' When a girl tried to share her pencil with me one day, I took it and stabbed her in the arm. I told the principal I was sorry and I got another chance. Then a boy asked me to dance and I kicked him in the balls. I'd get props for doing that in this me-too era, but back then I had a track record. See? I was the crazy girl. And at some point enough is enough. The straw that broke the camel's back was too heavy. I got kicked out."

"Everybody has a backstory," I said. "Nobody's perfect. Even those rich kids have their demons."

"The demons never leave people like me," Tempe said. "Good Kayla and bad Kayla. That's what the professionals would tell my parents. School after school, year after year, the same shit would go down. I'd have these awesome highs and these really bad lows. When I was high, I was the best at everything. Top of the class. Aced all my tests, did a ton of extracurriculars. Volunteered for charity. That bought me some leeway when my lows got really bad. But eventually people can't keep looking the other way when your lows hurt others. At that point, the experts have a completely different label for you entirely."

"Psychopath," I said.

"Yes. You're a psycho, and nobody can sweep your actions under the rug anymore. Doesn't matter how many A's you have or how many degrees. In high school I punched a kid so hard I broke his nose. His parents didn't press charges, so I skated on that. But in college I wasn't so lucky. Right before spring break my sophomore year I went to a party. I was on my meds. They made me sleepy, but they did a decent job of stabilizing my moods, you know? I went to the party and danced with some guys. Things were going well. I didn't have a boyfriend so I didn't feel any obligation to commit to one dance partner. I grinded on a couple of them, and they loved every minute of it. You know how stupid men get when they're hard. I didn't know which one to go home with. Then somebody spilled a drink on me."

Tempe pointed to her shirt and made a splattering motion with her free hand. I needed her to move a few inches closer so I could get in an uppercut.

"I ignored it the first few seconds," she said. "Then a switch flipped. Bad Kayla again. I couldn't help it. I pushed this poor gymnastics girl up against a wall. 'Why the fuck did you do that? Huh? You like spilling things on people, don't you?' The girl was scared shitless, but I was in the zone. I put my hands around her neck and choked the shit out of her. I would've killed her if a football player didn't step in and toss me aside like yesterday's garbage. Everybody else just stared. This was before Twitter and Snapchat and all that stupid shit. This time the girl's parents wanted to press charges, and I was arrested right on campus. I was put in a holding cell that smelled like refrigerated piss, and I went to court. My parents did every-thing they could to protect their baby. They got me a top lawyer, and he swung a deal. The charge was reduced from a felony battery with bodily harm to a misdemeanor disorderly conduct, and I got deferred prosecution. I did some community service hours and the case got tossed. Like it never happened. My lawyer even got the arrest expunged so nobody could see it. In theory. It went like that throughout college and law school. Arrests and fancy lawyers to make it all go away. Petty cases and bullshit misdemeanors. But I was delaying the inevitable."

"I'm sorry about yesterday," I said. "There was a method to my madness. You needed to be off the case. If I had known—"

Tempe took the gun away from her head and pointed it at my face. "That I'm who I am? You would have walked on eggshells around me? You would have been nicer to the crazy girl? That's what they all say when they're confronted with mental illness. It hits them in the face like a semi. What to do? Ignore the crazy person or coddle them too much? Rewind things or fast-forward so we can turn a new fucking leaf? You're just like all the rest. You act all funny and charming and pretend like you give a shit. Then the day comes when you make a million excuses and toss me aside like an old pair of shoes. That's how this story ends, and that's why I couldn't let it happen. Not when I'm the grandmaster of ceremonies."

"I'm not pretending. I don't want anything to happen to you. I care about you a lot. Put the gun down."

Tempe laughed—one of those maniacal laughs. "You think this is all about you, don't you? Your feelings and your regret. Did you actually think this was a love story? That we'd walk down the aisle, hold hands, read speeches and walk off into the sunset together? Damn, I knew boxers were fucked up in the head, but you take the cake. All that head trauma did a number. Vegas was right."

Tempe grinned then, and I saw Murdock's reflection telling me I'd been fucking played. I had wanted the fairytale ending this whole time. The revolving door of starts, stops, near-misses, and heartbreak in my life was getting old. Life wasn't a rom-com, but I wished it was. Most had happy endings.

Not here though.

Not now.

Not ever.

Tempe and I were through.

I said, "I came here for answers, and then I met you."

"How touching. Back to Vegas. Don't change the subject on me. You remember him right? The minute you got out, he told me you were coming. I didn't think much of it at first. Some boxer dude with no brain coming to look for Gertrude. You'd come in, ask some questions, I'd shoo you away, and that'd be that. The show goes on. Gertrude would stay missing, where she belonged. But you wouldn't fucking let it go."

"Stevenson wanted the best for everybody," I said. "She saw how talented you were and brought you along to fight the good fight." I was just spewing random bullshit now.

Tempe moved closer. "Gertrude would play the same game. Give all these platitudes and suck up. I remember the first time we met. I was just hired and she was trying to tell me how much of an asset I was and how much I'd grow with the firm. But she never let me handle my own cases. She hovered over everything. The other partners would give me space and let me do my own thing, but not her. She wouldn't let it go. *File this. Read this. Motion this up. Research this. We fucked up on this case, go convince the client to stick with us. Fudge your billables.* None of it was ever about litigating. I didn't go to law school to be a water girl my whole life. Maybe she saw herself in me. She was bipolar too, you know. Took a bunch of meds. But she was a superstar, so nobody cared about her lows. Winners get a pass. I'd contribute everything behind the scenes and I'd never get credit. She'd ride me all fucking day. And then you break. There's no other way around it."

"It's not like that. Please put the gun down."

"Shut the fuck up." Tempe was an arm's length away now. "She gets you out of prison and that same day invites me to her lake house in Wisconsin. Let's celebrate! Take a little break from it all. So I go all the way over there with Henri. It's a kick-ass lake house. All the bells and whistles. We eat, take in the scenery. I'm thinking we're turning the corner in our relation-ship. She's coming around. I'm staying the weekend, or at the very least for the night. Then the bitch comes out again. Pure Gertrude. She tells me you have to file this motion by tomorrow morning. 'It's super important. Get back to the office. The media's gonna get wind of it, we don't need them talking. But I need to talk to you about the case law first. I'll get the notes. Hold on.' She gets up, and that's when I had enough."

Tempe started crying again, and the tears flowed like Niagara Falls. She took the gun off me and waved it around.

I stayed put.

"Bad Kayla," she said. "Why is it always Bad Kayla? Dammit! I clubbed her in the back of the head with a fireplace poker. She didn't put up a fight, but she was still breathing. So I hit her again and again and again until her face looked like mashed potatoes. Fuck the motion. I waited till dark, got in one of her boats, and dumped her in the middle of the lake. Henri was inside when all this went down, but I think he knew the real deal. He pottied out of spite. When I got back to work I played it cool. I called 911 the next day. The office was going wild. Then I reamed out this bitch reporter who annoyed the hell out of everyone. Sticking her nose where it didn't belong. You have that in common. So my list expanded after that. Self-preservation is a beautiful thing."

"Monster," I said.

Tempe fired a shot into the side of the bed. I covered my head and fell to my knees. So much for my coping skills.

She laughed. "When Vegas told me you pussied out in the back of the van, I didn't believe him. The bad-ass champ, Lance Gedrin. But I see it now. My man never lies. He did a year bid in IDOC and came back speaking his truth. About Gertrude. They used to fuck, you know? And about the brotherhood. Blood. Higher purpose."

Tempe took off her watch, revealing a tattoo. *The* tattoo. The shark from hell.

"The devil's in the details," she said. "The boss hooked us up. Now we had a future, *comprende?*"

She fired another shot, and this one grazed my right shoulder. Either she was a shitty shot or she was warning me. I crawled on the floor, holding my shoulder. Sore, but no blood.

Tempe kicked me over, then said, "Come on. Get up."

I got up, and she kicked me down again. "Get up," she demanded.

This time I stayed down. Tempe pistol-whipped me. Blood poured down my face. I needed an opening. Any opening, and I could make it out alive.

"You gave me the Dapper file," I said. "You knew who it was."

"Bravo. Now we're getting somewhere." She twirled the gun like a baton.

"And I thought you liked deep dish."

"Please. I wanted to spit that shit out right in your face, but a gig is a gig. The Pako protestors were a twist I didn't expect, but it worked out. When my man says jump, I say how high. He calls the shots. He's really good in bed, so he gets a lot of leeway. Don't worry. We're in an open relationship, so I didn't technically cheat when we did the deed. Man, I felt nasty afterward though. I know who my man is. Plain and simple. And you know, too. You're just too stupid to piece the puzzle together."

I racked my brain, but nothing came out. Stress is the enemy of memory. I closed my eyes, not so much trying to piece it all together, just trying to make my final move.

My final play.

"You're a shitty investigator," Tempe said. "But I needed to make a splash and make partner. Gertrude won shit on appeal. On technicalities. She was never a great trial lawyer, but I was different. I brought you in, and lo and behold you have a case now too! And not just any case, but a high-profile shit show! Redemption! I'd be doing press conferences every day, and you'd be one step closer to life without parole. Romero never played nice. And then you fire me. For the whole world to see. The brotherhood never wanted to end you, but you pushed our hand. Asshole."

I put my hands up again. "What now?"

Tempe shook her head. "It's the end of the road. There's no going back after this."

"Turn yourself in and you can swing a deal for second-degree. Day-for-day credit."

She laughed. "They're gonna fry me. Illinois doesn't have the death penalty anymore, but the feds do. I crossed state lines for this one. The feds ain't dealing. And they'll send a message that court personnel are off-limits."

"Just do it," I said.

I'd known for a long time that a premature death was always in the cards for me. Boxing fucks up your brain. If the CTE didn't get me, the Parkinson's would, or a stroke or some other malady that afflicted the warriors of my profession. It comes with the territory. A gunshot would be a quicker way to go.

Tempe's gaze hardened. "Maybe in another life we could

have made it. You have an awesome smile and your body is heavenly. But people like me can't find true love. Nope. People aren't what they seem, Lance. Remember that. Gertrude too. Everybody has skeletons in their closet. Everybody has a night contract."

I charged at Tempe with everything I had left, and she fired.

And missed way right.

I tackled her into the nightstand. We fell to the floor and wrestled like we were at the Olympics. Tempe was damned strong, and she wouldn't let go of the gun. She fired another shot up close, and I felt pain flare up in my left hand. Another graze, but this one on my finger.

My luck was running out.

I threw a hard right and hit air, then a left hook which got a piece of the gun, knocking it to the floor. We both went for it, but my hand found it first.

It was too late for take-backs.

I pulled the trigger and blew Tempe's brains out.

41

My shoes were good, but the rest of my clothes didn't escape the impact. Bits of brain clung to my cottons like long-lost bedfellows. Tempe was gone, and so was I.

I stood there lost in translation for several minutes. A fog hung over me and kept saying hello. Everything was quiet yet everything was noisy. Stay away. Get away. Stop it. Please. No. Don't do that. My head fermented in a heavy vise grip. I saw Pontiac and bars and solitary and guards and shanks and gangs and blood and life and death and Murdock.

Then I snapped out of it.

I took one last look at Tempe and knew what I had to do.

I didn't have much time.

I took the gun and wiped it down so many times my wrist was numb.

Then I put it in the killer's hands. My actions were completely justified under the law. Self-defense. Muy bueno. But I wasn't going to stick around to tell my tale.

Even though Stevenson's place took up most of the top

floor, she still shared it with another tenant. The rich and famous enjoyed their privacy and do-not-disturb hangtags. After Tempe's shit-show, the cavalry was coming. I needed to get the hell out of Dodge, but I also needed the night contract.

Everybody has a night contract.

Everybody has skeletons in their closet.

Tempe was insane, but she knew Stevenson much better than I did. The contract, whatever the hell it was, held the keys to the kingdom. She wouldn't have said shit about it unless it was important.

I closed my eyes and used whatever brain cells I had left to get to the bottom of it. Think. The keys. The kingdom. The contract. The skeletons. My head hurt like hell, but I clenched my teeth and sucked it up. Eight seconds later I hit pay dirt. I opened my eyes. The home was one's castle. The home was the kingdom. The keys were *here*.

Stevenson had hid the contract where prying eyes could easily overlook it.

I ransacked the bedroom.

Nada.

I ransacked the guest bedrooms.

Nada.

I ransacked all the bathrooms and the kitchen and the closets.

Nada.

Two minutes and four seconds later I found it. I had a way of doing that. When the clock was ticking I came through in the clutch.

The keys were under one of the floorboards.

In the kitchen.

Loose and creaking and needing a lot of TLC.

For such a beautiful space, one wooden panel stood out. To

the naked eye the whole looked exquisite, but to the obsessive eye it was a travesty. It threw the space off balance.

I pulled out the floorboard, expecting the pizza rat from the Thai restaurant to greet me. Instead, I found a Ziploc baggie with dust all over it. There wasn't a contract in it or physical keys, but when I wiped away the dust there was something else.

A computer part.

I had seen one of these before at the Pontiac infirmary, but I was too busy chatting up one of the new nurses to ask about it. I took out the Jitterbug and searched for "computer hard part." A bunch of scantily clad ladies who would put Sandy to shame came up. I searched for "computer options." That brought up a bunch of articles on computers. Then I did "computer accessories," and I realized that the part was a USB drive. Storage for computer files. Plain and simple. Something was inside the USB, and I needed to figure out what. But I needed a computer. USB drives didn't play themselves.

I retraced my steps through Stevenson's place, looking for a computer this time. I found a laptop nestled under the couch. Stevenson must have been a multi-tasker, working while watching that big-ass screen. I pressed the power button, and the computer booted up. The screen showed one user: "G-baby." Stevenson really did have a lot of secrets. I pressed the arrow to the right of the flower icon and username.

It asked for a password.

Fuck.

I tried thirty-seven different combos. DOBs, addresses, hypothetical boxing dates, social security numbers or what I thought were social security numbers, A-list actors, B-list actors, and D-list actors. Then I went with court themes. Day of my trial. Date of my conviction. Date I met Stevenson in lockup. Date I won my appeal. Date I got out.

Date I got the news I'd be released.

Bingo.

I was Stevenson's favorite client.

And I was in.

Stevenson's computer was just as organized as her luxurious place. Instead of seeing a bunch of folders and diagrams and things, her desktop was empty. I popped in the USB and it buffered for two minutes before a folder flashed on screen.

I clicked the folder once. Then twice. More buffering.

Then a video played. An interview room that brought back my case and the avalanche of misdeeds courtesy of CPD's finest. This particular interview room took the cake when it came to shitty decor. One rusty table from the Stone Age, piss on the floors, two beetles on the walls, and three orange concrete chairs—one for the poor subject and two for the interrogators. The dick cops who made sure they got some kind of admission come hell or high water. They knew the score.

The video played for two minutes and showed nothing but the empty interview room.

Then Stevenson came in. She wore jeans and a baggy blue hoodie. Casual Friday at the station apparently. She sat where the interrogators sat. A kid walked in after. No more than thirteen, fourteen years old.

"Nice of you to join us, kiddo," Stevenson said. She had some papers in front of her and she scribbled as she talked. She didn't mention that the camera was rolling.

"I didn't do nothin'. Let me go home. I wanna call my momma." The kid looked green. A first-timer. He was in for a long night. But why was Stevenson playing cop?

"You're not going anywhere until you tell me why you stole from us." Stevenson stared the kid down like he had committed the biggest crime against humanity.

"Ma'am, I don't know what you're talking about. I didn't steal nothin'. I was with my friend in the park and he found—"

Stevenson sucker-punched him. The kid's nose busted open and the table was covered in red. Stevenson smiled the way Tempe did.

The door swung open, and Zarta joined her. This bastard was the other interrogator. They weren't wearing badges, and they didn't read the kid his Miranda rights. The needles pricked my stomach again.

"If you lie again," Zarta said, "I'll start with your hand." He made a cutting motion.

The kid's eyes went wide and he took three deep gulps of air.

Stevenson spoke next. "Tell us why you stole from us, honey, and everything will be cool."

The kid was terrified. "My buddy said there was a thousand in cash at the park bench on Harrison," he said. "Last two weeks, somebody was dropping it. So I went there, same spot the next week. And there's two thousand cash in a bag. Just sitting there. I'm poor, man. What do you want me to say? I took it."

"Do you think it's fair to take something that doesn't belong to you?" Zarta said.

"No, sir, I'm sorry. I'll pay it all back. I just used six hundred. I'll get the rest."

Zarta nodded at Stevenson. She turned back to the kid.

"Your honesty is greatly appreciated, but it comes with a price."

She pulled a gun from her pocket and shot the kid point-blank in the head.

Just like that.

Zarta took a handkerchief out of his breast pocket and wiped away some of the blood, then he turned to Stevenson and made out with her. "You're so fucking sexy, you know that? I knew you were special. But you know the drill."

Stevenson nodded, then took a bite out of the kid's arm. She looked back at Zarta and grinned as she chewed the piece of flesh.

I aged a hundred years watching the clip, but my metamorphosis was just beginning.

The video went dark for ten seconds. Then it started again, in the same interview room. No Zarta this time, and no kid either, but Stevenson was there, with a homeless man in a soiled white t-shirt. She interrogated him about stealing from an Irish pub in Andersonville. But the homeless man could barely string two complete sentences together. He was muttering along in mid-sentence when Stevenson blew his brains out too.

Stevenson didn't need Zarta for moral support this time.

I didn't see any timestamps, so I couldn't tell where this officially fell in her book of horrors.

This time she ate pieces of his brain.

One thing was crystal clear: Tempe was right. Everybody had skeletons in their closet. Everybody had a night contract. Stevenson had no moral compass. She moonlighted as Zarta's sick contractor. Lawyer by day, serial killer by night. Tempe's demise suddenly didn't feel as bad.

And the video kept on giving.

Same interview room. This time the subject was a pregnant woman. Not far along, but clearly expecting by the way she cradled her stomach with each step.

I didn't need a time stamp for this one. I already knew.

Because the woman was Amy Pako.

"Please," she begged. "I didn't do anything to you. Whoever you are, if you want money, I'll get it. I'll get it."

Stevenson was on her like a cheetah on the prowl. She pinned Pako to the wall, her elbow pressed against the poor woman's neck.

"One fucking move and I'll get the dogs."

Pako froze.

I was reeling.

Stevenson continued. "It's come to our attention that you've been diverting funds away from the brotherhood. Shame on you. You've lived a life of excess and privilege because the boss allowed you to take part in our cause. But taking advantage of the hand that feeds you is beyond the pale, missy. Now tell us where the funds are."

Pako shook her head. "I don't know what you're talking about. I didn't take anything. I play by the rules. Please."

The door opened. Zarta again.

And Pako smiled, with a look of relief.

"Baby," she said, "tell her this is all a mistake. I need to go home. I have to take my vitamins. You remember what the doctor said."

Zarta sat down. Stevenson released Pako, who went and sat across from him.

"I've had enough with women who only want to fuck and not contribute anything else to the relationship," Zarta growled. "I bring home the bacon and you lounge around and buy purses and scarves and whatever other bullshit you can waste my money on."

"No, baby, I—"

"Shut up. Where's my money?"

"I didn't take it!"

"Wrong answer."

"I swear, baby. Why would I take it when I'm getting so much from you already? You're an amazing man, baby. Please."

Zarta wasn't convinced, and neither was I. Pako would fail every polygraph known to man.

"We had a good run," Zarta said. "But I've moved on to greener pastures." He grinned at Stevenson, then nodded.

But Stevenson didn't move. Damn, the killer had a conscience.

"Do it," Zarta insisted.

"I'm not feeling well," Stevenson said.

"*Start* feeling well. I don't pay you for nothing."

"She has a baby. *Your* baby," Stevenson said.

"When you join the Zemun, you know the rules. Blood is blood. You wanted a family? You got one. The girl with nothing became everything. You wanted to be the best in the game, and you got there. Impressing society on my dime. We're far past exceptions to the rules."

Stevenson folded her arms. "It's a baby. Don't do this."

Zarta laughed. "You weren't bothered with the kid."

"This is different."

Zarta closed his eyes. "Evil with a conscience. Have it your way."

He leaned toward Pako, and she screamed. But he just shook his head, rose to his feet, opened the door, and said, "Vegas."

A man stepped in. His back was to the camera, so I couldn't see his face. And he didn't say a single word—he just took out a knife and slit Pako's throat.

Zarta turned to Stevenson. "There's no going back. You had a night contract, and it's hereby been rescinded. The Zemun will figure out your fate in due time. I suggest you atone for your sins."

He turned to Vegas. "Get rid of the bitch and pin it on the asshole who lost me ten million with Goluka. Cost me my wife and kids."

Vegas picked up Pako's body and carried it out of the room.

And that's when I got a clear view of his face.

Vegas was the damn kid from the tattoo shop.

42

I found a cab ten seconds before the cops showed. As I rolled away from the building, the security dude had both eyes open now and was directing Chicago's finest to the freight elevator. They'd find a doozy upstairs.

I paid no attention to the driver this time, and twelve minutes later I arrived at my destination: Sal's gym. It was packed with the after-work crowd. A bunch of amateurs throwing awkward combinations at a heavy bag that always seemed to get the better of them. The resolutioners left around February or March, while the regulars stayed but never quite improved. Part of it was lack of talent, but the other part of it was Sal's kid. When Sal's kid took over daily operations, Sal's coaching had disappeared. Gone were the days when he'd take an energetic chap under his wing and guide him up the boxing food chain. The tutelage was gone. The patience, too. Either you had it or you didn't. No room for projects. As I looked around the gym I saw a couple kids with decent technique, but without proper guidance they'd go astray and never make it to the promised land.

"You're getting fat, my boy."

I turned to find Sal standing behind me, with his five-seven skeletal frame, bald head, and cowboy mustache. He hadn't changed one bit.

"I've been cutting the silver dollar pancakes," I said.

Sal seemed destroyed to the core, but he let it pass. He put his hand on my shoulder. "My boy, I knew you'd be back. My stupid son said you came by the other day. But he didn't tell me nothing till this morning. I wanted to punch him right in the kisser." Sal was ever the dramatist.

"That's okay," I said. "He's a very busy man. And we don't want to ruin his chances with the ladies by giving him a shiner."

Sal laughed. "Too busy to tell me the champ is here? You *made* this gym, boy! It's because of you that we even have anybody who wants to pay a fee to use this shitty place. And you can forget the ladies. My son is forever stupid in that department. He's been looking for his match for forty years. Bah."

"This is a very special place," I said.

"It has great sentimental value," Sal agreed. "I refuse to upgrade it like those sissy spots."

"You can at least get some Wi-Fi. This place is tragic without it."

"Wi-what? Boy, you're turning into the rest of them."

The two kids that I was eyeing for talent came up and asked for an autograph.

Wrong move. Sal snapped at them. "You think this gym is for staring? Nobody becomes a champ like that. Put in the work, and maybe you can hold this man's jockstrap. You think he fucked around when he came in here? Huh?" He motioned them toward the heavy bag. "Maybe I'll convince him to sign later."

The kids ran back to the bag and put in some more work.

"They seem promising," I said.

"So many kids come in here from the streets. No mothers. No fathers. Homeless. They have the spirit, but they don't have the restraint. Believe it or not, there are rules in this game."

I laughed. "Beat somebody's brains in. Pretty simple."

Sal shook his head. "You stupid, still never learned. We're lucky we held on to the title so long. Boxing is an art. How many times I have to tell you that? You can't just knockout all day. Bam. Bam. Bam. Doesn't work like that."

I'd heard the speech a million times before, but I enjoyed hearing it again. It brought me back to the ring and to the camaraderie and the highest of highs and lowest of lows. Above all else, it brought me back to the look on Sal's face every time I'd ignore his advice and still kick my opponent's ass. Ha.

Sal looked me up and down the way a drill sergeant does his morning recruits. "You been training hard?"

"Yeah."

"Good. Keep it that way."

"I've got a lot left in the tank."

Sal smiled. "The game's different nowadays. But if we do this again, we do this right."

"Same shit talkers. Can't hit what you can't see." I did some feints, and Sal put his mitts on and threw some punches like we were in the tunnel getting ready to be walked out to the ring.

Then Sal said, "Are you ready for tomorrow?"

"Since the day I went in."

"Who's your lawyer?"

"Some dude Mark says is the best in the city. Wesley. I forgot his last name."

Sal wrinkled his nose at Mark's name, but nodded. "They took your life away the first time. They better not take it away again. I almost didn't survive it. I thought I had a heart attack, but the doctor said it was all that stress. Panic attacks. Thank

God my Maria stayed strong with me. Especially after those first few times."

I understood. Unlike my rep, Sal had visited me regularly at Pontiac until the attacks got the better of him. I told him I was thankful for the visits, but to stay away till I got out.

"Things are going to be different this time," he said. "I've been ready for twelve years. Revenge is a dish best served cold."

Sal was always in my corner, but I wasn't about to tell him everything that had been going on lately. I doubted he'd be interested in how all the women in my life were dead, two were cannibals, and how I'd fucked up my first legit job on the outside. One day I'd give it all to the old man, but for now I'd preserve his systolic blood pressure. So all I said was, "Can't wait."

After that I went to the locker room. The old-school vibe from the outside carried into the man cave, with one long rusty bench that ran the length of the whole floor. The lockers were ten times smaller than most because Sal didn't believe in bringing a bunch of things to workout. A bunch of things meant distractions and fucking around. Bring your gloves and your wraps. Those were Sal's golden rules.

I walked past the lockers and went straight to the showers. One was out of order and the other two were so old that nobody dared chance their life with them. The water flow couldn't be trusted and the temperature couldn't be regulated. More hard knocks from Sal. No wonder the locker room was empty.

Which was great for me.

I knew my mission.

Right next to the shower that was out of order was a small window, and right under the window was what looked like a secret cupboard. When I asked Sal about it years ago he said it was from prior ownership. The gym had a serious rat problem back in the day, and the cupboard trapped them nicely. Fill it

with cheese, poison, or whatever the experts used, and voila—
problem solved.

I used to use the cupboard to store some of the finest maga-
zines in the world. Away from Mama's prying eyes. The large
Gorilla tape surrounding all four corners signaled *out of order*
in any language.

Now I needed it for something completely different.

I took one last look around the place to make sure there
were no spies. Then I took out the baggie and the USB and
shoved them inside.

And I grabbed what I came for and put it in my pocket.

I shut the cupboard and locked it with the makeshift string
thing Sal had put there. I walked back out of the locker room,
signed for the up-and-comers, and headed out.

I had some unfinished business.

43

The neon sign outside Tony's Tats was half green and half orange. Four of the letters hung down at a weird angle that screamed lawsuit. When I walked in, Fat Tony was inking up a Cuban girl's ass. It was a floral design, and I admired the artistry.

Fat Tony smiled. "One of my very best designs."

"Totally," the Cuban girl said. I suspected she could shake that ass better than Sandy, but for once she had to keep it still.

"What brings you back, Flintstone?" Tony asked.

"The kid," I said. "What stupid shit is he getting into today?"

"Probably jacking off in back. Talk some sense into him, will ya?"

I smiled. "Will do."

As Fat Tony went back to work on the Cuban girl's ass, adding more shades of red to the flower petals, I walked past a row of dog chains and found the back room. When I pushed the door open I was greeted by an odor that rivaled that of a hundred pizza rats. The back doubled as storage for both needles and random knick-knacks that were used during the Cold War. They came in twenty-eight different shapes and sizes. And the boxes that housed them were alphabetized with foreign scrawl.

I stood there for a moment marveling at the storage capacity. Fat Tony was a hoarder, but a clever one.

Then Vegas said, "Ah, the indestructible Mr. Gedrin."

He still had the nose ring and the kiddie voice, but he seemed bigger now.

"The last twelve years have been super kind to you," I said.

"Exuberance and charisma," he replied. "But the eyes don't lie, boxer man. I've seen it all, even if my skin says otherwise. Been on this earth longer than most. It's a blessing and a curse."

I stared Vegas down like he was my tasty prey in the ring. Tyson used to beat his opponents the moment he walked out to the music. The stare slayed all.

"Pray that you come out of here with a blessing," I said.

Vegas laughed. "I had you at the park, boxer man. Hell, I had you here, when you came in with my side piece. She did a beautiful job. You kept thinking with your dick and all she had to do was show you the way. Make you think you were on our trail. Keep you alive so you get fucked by the courts again. We had our brother on the bench ready to lay down the law, but you went off-script."

"I should do standup."

Vegas cracked his knuckles. "How do you want to die?"

"Eating a double cheeseburger on the beach. With truffles," I said. "Better scenery for the first responders."

"You're more of a pain in the ass than I thought."

"Gracias."

Vegas walked in a half circle on his side, and I did the same on mine. The jitters before a fight were always palpable. I wouldn't have it any other way.

"It's a shame you won't be able to enjoy my club again," Vegas said.

I did some neck circles. "Sandy is an exemplary employee. I hope you pay up for good talent."

"Whores are a dime a dozen. They all know how it works. Get out of line a bit and they're back on the streets sucking dick for ten bucks a pop."

"Shame," I said.

"Indeed."

Then Vegas pounced.

I was expecting it. Street fights don't follow the Nevada Athletic Commission Rules and Regs.

But I still got kneed in the face.

Vegas might have been half my size, but what he lacked in the physical department he more than made up for in the MMA department. He fought in the octagon, while I languished away in the boxing ring.

I staggered back, blood pouring from my nose. I'd need a rhinoplasty when this was all said and done. I wiped away some of the mess, but the needles in my stomach kept saying hello.

"That all you got, old man?" Vegas said.

I crowded him, throwing body shots. One. Two. Three. Four.

They all hit air.

Vegas was fucking good, and I was in for a long night.

Vegas got me with a left hook to the jaw.

Then a roundhouse kick to the left ear.

Dammit.

Part of a fighter's DNA is the ability to take superhuman amounts of punishment and keep going. The other part is the ability to throw down in return. My ears were ringing and my equilibrium was off. I saw two of Vegas. Then one. Then two again. Maybe I did have an expiration date in this game.

"That jaw of yours just couldn't stay shut," Vegas said. "We let that bitch move on with her life after she failed us. We told her she'd be looking over her shoulder forever, but it was the price to pay for getting out of the brotherhood. You took the fall. And she wouldn't let up. She's a killer." He danced around me. "She got cute with some motions and your ass is back out. Do we finish the job? Or do we let it be? I've always been a work first kinda guy. Blood is blood. But the boss had a sweet spot for her ass. Even though I tapped it first. Let it be. But you went to that cunt reporter. Too close for comfort now. If I'd known you were in the van I would have sprayed a hundred more bullets with my boy Howie."

"Zarta has all the balls, but he lets Minnie Mouse pick up all the scraps," I said.

Vegas didn't appreciate the visual. He charged and got me clean with three kicks to the stomach. I doubled over. The needles were so sharp, my insides probably resembled an eccentric mosaic. I needed my equilibrium back. I didn't know MMA. But I knew the streets. I'd been through a million sparring sessions all over town. Sal's methods were king.

When Vegas geared up for another kick, I rolled toward him, cut the distance. That threw him off his game. His feet were in mud for a second.

And I used the confusion to grab his throat.

His eyes rolled back in his head as I lifted him off the ground.

Vegas might have been an adult, but he felt like a featherweight in that moment. I lifted him high over my shoulders, laughing at how easy it was. The asshole talked all hard, but he couldn't finish the job.

But pride cometh before the fall.

Vegas was game.

He slammed both his fists on the top of my head. I lost my grip, and when Vegas came down he kicked me in the balls. I fell, and my head bounced off the concrete. He picked me up by my hair and threw me into a box of vases. It was sealed tight, so at least I didn't greet the shards.

"I should have fed you to a colony of rats," Vegas said. "And dunked your fucking head in the courthouse bathroom."

"I shouldn't trust untrustworthy women," I said.

"You know what her last words were?" Vegas said.

"Tempe's?"

"No. That bitch is crazy. Pako, boxer man."

"Halitosis," I said.

Vegas got me with a one-two combo and more blood poured out of my mouth. "She held her stomach and looked me in the eye and said, 'Tell Johnnie.' He was the baby daddy. Went AWOL on assignment and almost got his whole platoon killed. She hooked up with that asshole and wanted him to parent the kid. Can you believe that?"

I was too fucked up to understand the nuances of Vegas's story. Maybe with clearer faculties I'd have agreed with him. But I was seeing four of him now. I shook my head, but that number was set in stone.

Vegas laughed and threw an uppercut.

There comes a time during every fight when the cumulative damage does you in. Endurance falters. Legs feel like Jell-O. You stop listening to your corner and do stupid shit.

I was done. Vegas's punches weren't hard, but a sum is always greater than its parts.

Everything went black.

Vegas laughed.

One.

Sal.

Two.
Henri.
Three.
Tempe.
Four.
Stevenson.
Five.
Henri.
Six.
Pancakes.
Seven.
The keeper who banished me.
Eight.
Sal.
Nine.
The Cuban girl's ass.
Ten.
Mom.
"Get your ass up, champ! Up! Up! Up! Now!"
My eyes flew open and I got to my feet.
Vegas smiled. "You have a lot of fucking brain damage."
"Ditto."
Vegas charged me, trying to do a leaping Superman punch.

I took the brass knuckles out of my pocket and threw a hard right just as Vegas lowered his center of gravity. Mounds of flesh tore off his skin as he crumpled to the ground. I went to ground and pound, and this time it was a crony-free experience.

Left. Right. Left. Right. Left. Right.

The brass knuckles made Lopez's cousin look beautiful by comparison. It went like that for three minutes. Vegas wouldn't be confused for a kid anymore. It was too late for Amy Pako, but not for her family.

I checked his pulse.

Si.

I found some utility ropes and tied Vegas to a chair. I wasn't an expert in secure fastening, but I used nine different ropes and nine different loops. It'd take a polar bear to break it all up.

Then Fat Tony came in.

"Give me one good reason why I shouldn't call the cops," he said.

"One more fucking step and you'll be next," I said. "Keep tatting that girl's ass and don't forget the stem."

Fat Tony hightailed it out of Dodge.

Vegas stirred. "Zarta won't forget this."

I knocked him back out with a left hook. "Too late."

I took my phone out of my pocket and stopped the recording. For a flip phone, it really got the job done. Who needed all that fruit? Technology was amazing.

I watched my quarry for a minute.

Then I called Decker.

When she picked up I said, "I've got him. Come give him some Colorado love."

I gave her the address, and I never set foot in another tattoo shop again.

44

Three hours later I was in a boat on a lake in a Wisconsin town I'd never heard of before. The water was quiet and in the distance the lights from a rustic lake house pinged off the water like serpents trying to find their home. I fully expected a grand finale of lights closer to bedtime. Some writer or aspiring creative would make sure of it. Which would be much appreciated, since I didn't bring a flashlight.

Neither did Murdock.

I'd bribed him to come along with two trips to Portillo's. On the house. Murdock loved Italian beef. But since he was my designated driver he chose the intervals of consumption. So we stopped once on the way over and stayed for fifty-six minutes. I had a milkshake and a fine piece of chocolate cake. Comfort food to soothe my aching joints. Maybe on the way back I'd succumb to the beef.

"You a swimma, my brotha?" Murdock said.

"I can go forward, but not backwards," I said.

"That's a butterfly stroke. I mean a breaststroke. You do that, you good around here. Water don't seem too deep."

Listening to Murdock analyze the properties of water was like listening to a carney waxing poetic about cures for cancer. I shook my head. The swimming gene had passed me by early in life and I never looked back. I doubted I'd be able to pick it up now with needles, a swollen face, and the remnants of pain meds in my system.

No bueno.

I had no idea what our exact coordinates were, but the lake wasn't that big. If I had to guess I'd say it was about the size of a hockey rink. Hockey was cool.

"Let's start there," I said, nodding to what I thought was the middle of the lake. Murdock was the boat operator and I was the pointer.

He shook his head as he steered. "My brotha, when you searching for treasure do you start at Point A or Point Q?"

"Depends where the dragon is hiding."

"Imagine that. Two cons boating and looking for a dead lawyer. This shit for the book," Murdock said.

Life had a way of bringing people together in the weirdest moments. I wanted my advance, and I got it—and then some.

"*Carpe diem*," I said.

Murdock found the middle of the lake and stopped the boat. I stared out at the water, hoping for a serial killer to float up to the surface. Nada. I knew this was the place though, because Murdock's recon on Tempe said as much. The water didn't seem too deep, but the only way to find out was to take a dive. Awesome.

"Let's wait for the rain, my brotha," Murdock said. "Pressure pushes things upwards."

"It's not raining till next week," I said.

Murdock scratched his head and analyzed the water from ten different angles. For a minute I thought he was an actual topographer. Then he got tired and pulled out a pack of smokes.

"This gonna be my downfall," he said.

"Get the patch," I said.

"That shit bogus. Consumer deception."

I nodded. I'd known a lot of people on the inside who had no success with the patch. The only way to quit sometimes was to get the cancer scare from the doc. Maybe Murdock would follow suit, but he could still bench a mountain and showed no signs of slowing down.

I stared out at the lake one more time. I knew what I had to do. I'd made the promise all the way back in Idaho. I owed Stevenson that much. No matter the circumstances. She'd fought for me, gave me life. And she fell—like all mortals do. When the books were written about her, there wouldn't be an asterisk by her name. It'd be one long flowing narrative. It'd be the best- looking parabola of all time. Better than my love life.

I took my shirt off, my jeans, and my socks. I folded them nicely and stretched my back out. It hurt like a bitch.

"What do you bench?" Murdock asked.

"Less than you," I said.

Murdock took a drag of his cigarette. "You slacking."

He was right.

Not about the slacking.

But about the conditions.

Right then the raindrops came. Two or three at first, then a torrential downpour. Murdock ditched the smokes.

"If I'm not back up in two minutes grab me. Punch me in the stomach and I'll come to."

"Boy, if you're not up in two minutes those courts ain't never gonna touch you."

I smiled.

Then I dove into the water.

Hell, Murdock was right again.

45

The next morning, I was at 26th Street. The sharks were lined up two blocks away and their news antennas stretched so high Jack couldn't scale that beanstalk. The gawkers discovered their purpose again, the deputies had less mandible pain, and the line inside was three-eighths the size of the last time. I whisked through the metal detectors in one minute flat, and I didn't pay to house my phone. Agent-lawyers come in handy sometimes. And they have more durable pockets.

"We're late," Sims said.

"We have twenty-four minutes," I said.

"Wesley wants to go over everything. You have a tendency to miss appointments."

"Cool." Last night on Sims's couch I'd spilled everything. I told him about the USB and what Sal's hours were. While I was smelling like seaweed a bunch of suits kicked down Sal's door and descended upon the locker room. He almost knocked all their asses out. Then Sims got Andrews involved. A million calls were made, and for the first time ever court made me happy.

Things were looking up.

But it ain't over till it's over.

I repeated that in my head as I got on the elevator and packed in with the sardines again. Sims and I got out on five and met with Andrews right in the same spot where Tempe and I had been a couple days before. The courthouse was quiet and traffic was light. How times change.

Andrews shook my hand. "Mr. Gedrin, this has been an interesting ride, but I'm glad it's going to work out in our favor. Aruba didn't want to let me go, but that's all right." He flashed his pearly whites. His suit looked like three million bucks.

Sims said, "Don't say anything when your case is called. Let Wesley do his job. Got it?"

I said, "What if I want to congratulate my legal team?"

Andrews's face was red. I couldn't tell if it was from his penchant for swinging the bottle or because he wanted to choke me.

"Shut the fuck up and let me handle it," he said.

"Fair enough."

We stood there for a few minutes and made small talk. Andrews asked about some of my fights, and I asked about some of his high-profile cases. He loved drug jury trials and he reminisced at times about Stevenson. I stayed silent through all the boring parts and piped in through all the important parts. Sims tried to insert some jokes into the conversation, but they fell flat.

A few minutes later I heard Carpetopoulos's squeaky cart. He looked like he'd gained thirty pounds in the last forty-eight hours. His hopes for the governor's mansion were vanishing quicker than a teenager's bank account. Since my team didn't want me to talk in court, I figured out of court was fine.

"Good morning Mr. Carpetopoulos. Loved your press conference the other day. Wish I'd had a big bag of Planters peanuts to go along with it."

I could tell he wanted to kill me, but there were too many witnesses. He gritted his teeth and went into the courtroom with his minions.

Sims laughed and said, "Showtime."

As I walked into court, I could tell it paid to have a real lawyer. The minute the judge saw us he yelled, "Ah, Mr. Andrews, what case do you have?"

Romero wasn't on the bench anymore. The brass name-plate read *Hickory Hanson*. I'd never heard of the guy in my life, but with Romero out, the dominos were falling in my favor.

Andrews smiled. "Lance Gedrin."

Hanson knew that beforehand, but he was playing it up for the sharks. He shuffled some papers, grabbed my file, and said, "Lance Gedrin."

I walked down the aisle, all eyes fixed to me like glue. I heard the whispers and snickers, but this time the vibe was better.

"Parties," the judge said, "please identify yourselves for the record."

"Evangelos Carpetopoulos for the people." Cry me a river.

"Wesley Andrews for Mr. Gedrin, who's present in court and to my left."

I noticed that none of the deputies were behind me like last time. Andrews was real good.

Hanson read some notes from the court file. "Well, it's come to my understanding that there have been some recent developments in this case. Not the least of which was the removal of a judge from the bench for conduct unbecoming. Just another day at 26th Street, I guess. State."

Hanson wasn't going to do all the work. He wanted the wannabe governor to have his moment. Ha ha.

Carpetopoulos shrank five feet and looked like he'd been demoted to the D-league. He glanced back toward the suits who flanked him, then faced the judge and cleared his throat.

"Your Honor, first I'd like to say for the record that my office takes criminal prosecutions very seriously. We prosecute thousands of cases every day in courthouses all over Cook County. We work very hard on behalf of all the citizens of Cook County. We advocate tirelessly for the victims of crimes to make our society a better place for everybody. Your Honor knows the history of Mr. Gedrin's case. I think most of the nation knows at this point. My office felt we had the evidence to proceed in a retrial for Mr. Gedrin and we stated our intent—"

"Get to the point, counselor," Hanson said. "I've got a full call."

Andrews smiled.

"Judge, while we made clear we were going to retry Mr. Gedrin, it has come to my attention that there is new exculpatory evidence that implicates other individuals in the death of Amy Pako. Three of them are due in bond court very soon. We have video evidence of the actual murder of Ms. Pako, and this video has been authenticated by CPD and other law enforcement agencies that were assisting in the investigation. It's quite clear at this point that Mr. Gedrin did not murder Ms. Pako. This has been a whirlwind for the family, but I cannot ethically and in good conscience proceed against an innocent man. As such, it will be motion-state *nolle pros* on all charges."

"DDT, and I'm tendering a written demand," Andrews said.

"You can't demand on a nolle, Mr. Andrews, but well done. State, I don't think you're finished."

Hanson stared bullets at Carpetopoulos, who looked absolutely confused. Then it registered on his face.

He nodded. "And for the record, on behalf of my office and all the citizens of Illinois and Cook County, I'd like to apologize to Mr. Gedrin. He's spent an inordinate amount of time in custody for a crime he didn't commit. We can't give him those years back, but I hope my apology does something to heal the wounds."

Whatever, hombre. I still hate loud carburetors.

Judge Hanson turned to me. "Mr. Gedrin, you're free to go. You have no further business with the court. And if you get back in the ring again, kick some ass for all of us, will ya?"

I smiled. "I sure will."

Hanson called another case, and that was it. I walked back down the aisle, and a Goth dude with dreads walked toward the bench. People were saying a whole bunch of things, but I didn't hear any of it. When I got back out to the hall, Andrews smiled and told me to call him anytime, then shuffled off to do media downstairs.

And then there were two.

Me and Sims.

"Well, that was fun," Sims said.

"Yep. Let's get back to work."

"You have to get your licenses back and get cleared. You could've passed a physical five years ago, but hell, now it's a whole different story."

"I need a camp."

"No shit."

I told Sims I'd swing by later to pick up my things. And then I'd be on my way. For a little while anyway. Sims would figure out the rest.

Sims handed me my Jitterbug. "Get this piece of shit outta here."

I pocketed it and smiled. "You shyster. I can't have a phone in the building."

"After what they've put you through? Fuck 'em."

We bro-hugged, and Sims was gone.

I stared out the window overlooking the jail. It still looked like shit, but at least I didn't have to get up close and personal with it anymore. Freedom is a beautiful thing.

I took a piss in the same bathroom as last time. Vegas's message was gone, but in its place was a pair of carefully crafted tits that would give Fat Tony a run for his money.

I took the elevator back down with the rest of the sardines.

And instead of taking a right toward the exit, I took a left.

46

Central Bond Court happened every day in room 100. On weekends, hearings were heard at 1:30. But rules were meant to be broken. Especially in Cook County. Bond court was happening at ten a.m. today, and the sharks were all over it. They filled the front rows of the courtroom, scribbling away faster than junkies on speed. There was one lone camera set up; the sharks had gotten permission in advance and would likely have it for the rest of the case. I took a seat in the very back of the gallery and waited. Six people asked me for autographs, but the deputies shooed them away. They smiled at me.

Three minutes later Judge Adam Sase took the bench. He looked like Romero, but with a little more swag. He got right down to business.

"Eduardo Zarta, co-defendants James Dapper, Howie Cajokovic."

The sharks in front were having a field day.

A dividing wall separated the gallery from the bench. Defendants were brought from the back lockup door. Like an assembly line. One waited against the wall. Another waited farther up. And another was all the way at the bench with his public pretender. At least, that was how it usually went. But Sase wanted all three brought to the bench at the same time, which required a wall of deputies behind them to prevent escape. If they somehow got through the wall, then there was another deputy by the door leading back out to the hallway. And if they somehow got past that deputy, *I'd* be waiting to knock the shit out of all three of them.

The deputies brought out the three men of the hour—all of them cuffed. So much for escape. I could see that Decker had done a number on Vegas after I left. His throat had so many marks on it, he looked like one of those crazies from *The Exorcist*. And I knew that Decker's work hadn't stopped there—she'd reamed out Chicago's finest so bad that they'd worked overtime to round up the other defendants in record time.

Cajokovic was the wannabe Carton. Maybe he'd find a new shelving gig at the jail.

And Zarta was the wannabe John Gotti. His Canali suit was faded and didn't have a pocket square. He wore no belt, and his Oxfords had no laces. For safety reasons. Zarta wrinkled his nose when he came out.

After verifying their names, Sase said, "Gentlemen, you're charged with murder, conspiracy to commit murder, kidnapping, fraud, unlawful restraint, and a bunch of misdemeanors. I'm not going to go through them. There's a finding of probable cause. State."

A young bubbly state's attorney gave a long-winded proffer that included my name at least five times. With each mention, the gallery whispered and the deputies held order. Vegas and Zarta had private lawyers with wrinkly suits, and Cajokovic had a public pretender.

Sase gave all of them no bail.

I smiled.

Good luck in county, motherfuckers.

Zarta's eyes caught mine for a split second, then the deputies pushed him and told him to move his ass as he was ushered away to his new home.

As I left the courtroom, I ignored the reporters beside me. I took in the same photos on the walls and the same sounds and the same people and then finally made it out of the courthouse.

Andrews was gone.

That left me.

The star of the hour.

The sharks were ready and the flashes almost blinded me. It was a feeding frenzy that would make Jaws jealous.

"What are your plans next?" someone shouted.

And right then and there, at 10:16 a.m., I played nice for a change.

"I'm getting some pancakes," I said. "The fluffier the better."

I caught a bus and got the hell out of Dodge.

47

The Space Needle stands over 605 feet tall in the center of Seattle, Washington. The tower's saucer-shaped top is over 500 feet and offers a beautiful 360-degree panoramic view of downtown and the Cascades. Built in 1962, the landmark is one of the most photographed places in the world.

I did well to have it on my bucket list.

Tickets are around forty bucks. Less if you bundle it with other attractions in the area.

I got in free.

The mayor of Chicago pulled some strings with the honchos in Seattle, and they closed down the place for an infamous exoneree boxer dude.

The staff almost didn't let me bring in Henri, but when I told him he was a service animal it was all good. Henri and I had made a lot of progress over the last couple days. He no longer ate the cuffs of my jeans, and he'd stopped pissing on my things. He'd gained three pounds of muscle and snored at a decibel level that didn't disturb me. He was cool.

The view was everything I'd thought it would be and then some. The circumstances that had brought me here might have been off-script, but the journey made all the difference.

The glass floor below my feet started rotating, and Henri barked.

"That's the Loupe," one of the staffers said. "The world's first and only rotating glass floor."

Henri chased the moving panels.

"Where's the cafe?" I asked.

"The Atmos Cafe is on the upper observation level, Mr. Gedrin. Right this way."

We found an elevator. At the top, a special meal had already been prepared for us. So many plates and so many sides. Drinks and desserts too. I would have tipped the cooks something crazy, but I'd given Decker the rest of my advance for her sister's funeral.

Henri sat at my feet, begging. I gave him a tiny piece of sausage and felt something new course through every fiber of my body. It couldn't be quantified, and it couldn't be taken away. But it was real.

Fatherhood.

AUTHOR'S NOTE

Thanks for reading! I hope you enjoyed the Gedrin universe just as much as I enjoyed writing it. I would greatly appreciate it if you would leave a review on Amazon. Reviews allow more readers to find Gedrin, and this ultimately allows me to keep writing stories that I hope will leave an indelible footprint in our literary world.

—Greg

ACKNOWLEDGMENTS

Thank you to my team. Writing may be a solitary endeavor, but publishing is certainly a collective one. Thank you to my beta readers Bailee Myers, Miranda Niles, and Samantha Petitti. Your early insights really helped whip Gedrin into shape.

Thank you to my editor David Gatewood for making my prose shine. Thank you to my proofreader Donna Rich for snagging those pesky typos. Thank you to my cover designers at Deranged Doctor Design. I'm blown away by all the Gedrin covers and this one is no different.

And of course thank you to all those who have shaped my writing indirectly in some way. It's impossible to mention everybody here, but y'all know who you are.

ALSO BY GREG GOUNTANIS

THE LANCE GEDRIN SERIES

The Night Contract (Lance Gedrin #1)

The Fink (Lance Gedrin #2)

The Loran (Lance Gedrin #3)

The Jobber (Lance Gedrin #4)

The Lance Gedrin Box Set (Books 1-4)

SNEAK PEEK THE FINK (GEDRIN #2)

Henri made friends with the monkeys. He stood at attention like a Navy SEAL at roll call and got down on all fours. He whined and rolled on his back. He stuck his tongue out. If Henri were getting graded, he'd pass with flying colors. Know thy audience. Play to the crowd. The monkeys were fans. Plain and simple. They cheered and tapped their craniums.

Henri held his right paw up like a flamingo and looked back at me. I nodded and gave him more leash. I was a chill fur padre, and Henri had a service pass. Not many Dobermans could say their old owner was a serial killer and their new owner gave people concussions for breakfast. Legally. But truth is stranger than fiction sometimes. And laughing is the best game in town. Henri and I were Laurel and Hardy without the monochrome. We went with the flow till the flow had other plans.

Henri licked the glass, and the monkeys made farting noises from their side of things. The Oregon Zoo had hundreds of exhibits, but Henri was on a mission. He pawed at the glass and barked twice. The monkeys cheered. Two minutes later the show fizzled out, and Henri bid adieu. We trudged on no worse for the wear.

I looked at the zoo directory and Henri licked all the passersby. I didn't have a game plan, but I had three choices. Curtain 1: See every exhibit in the place. Start at point A and make it all the way to point Z. Curtain 2: Close my eyes and wherever my pinkie taketh me I shall go. Curtain 3: See the best damned exhibit. Quality over quantity. I racked my brain long and hard, and decided.

Quality.

I smiled and hung a left at the fork in the path. Freedom was muy bueno. When you spend twelve years in a box for a murder you didn't commit and come seconds away from getting a three-drug cocktail that will stop your heart forever, you appreciate choices. Both big and small. Clean air, too.

And in a few hours, I'd be on a plane back to business. I'd be in Sin City with one simple task: kick Nik Juko's ass. He was a punk, but he was also the number-one contender for the heavyweight title. On paper, anyway. My agent, Mark Sims, couldn't get me the big fight after my Chicago legal woes, but he got me the next best thing: a number-one contender fight in forty-eight hours. Beat Juko, get my title shot. Lose to Juko...and I'd be delivering gluten-free pizzas somewhere.

After I kicked Juko's ass, the plan was to make it to Horseshoe Bend. Numero tres on my ever-expanding bucket list. As much as I enjoyed beating people's brains in, I was a nomad. And a nomad couldn't rest on his laurels or play house. Evolve. Live. Learn.

That's the way to do it, hombre.

I walked past three very boring exhibits, two boring exhibits, and one slightly less boring exhibit. Then I found it.

The African painted dog. One of the best creatures in the whole damned zoo.

But the people by the exhibit were paying no attention to the painted dog. They were mobbed around something else, and I heard a frightened gasp.

Then the crowd broke for a second and I saw a man lying in a pool of blood.

GET The Fink Now on Amazon

JOIN GREG'S NEWSLETTER

For the latest updates on Greg's writing, sign up for his newsletter at: https://dashboard.mailerlite.com/forms/1415379/150624884207126495/share

ABOUT THE AUTHOR

Greg Gountanis writes mysteries and thrillers filled with a lot of action, wit, and courtroom drama. When he's not writing, he's lawyering. For over a decade, Greg's worked as a public defender in Chicago.

Get the latest news on Greg's books at www.greggountanis.com and on social media.

f facebook.com/GregGountanisAuthor

a amazon.com/stores/author/B08P1C58RR

youtube.com/greggountanis

www.ingramcontent.com/pod-product-compliance
Lightning Source LLC
Chambersburg PA
CBHW031612240626
47153CB00002B/735